Snubbed

Zane had turned back and was staring down after the college boys, her face displaying the same subtle disappointment as Carrie's voice.

"Don't worry about those boys," Mary Beth said, bolstering Zane. "The blond one is the only one who's cute. Besides, boys like that make me nervous."

"I know." Zane relaxed. Mary Beth had restored her confidence. "They make me nervous, too." She pretended to faint, then tickled Mary Beth. Carrie started laughing, too. "That's the whole point."

**Other Point paperbacks
you will want to read:**

point

Sweet Sixteen

Linda A. Cooney

SCHOLASTIC INC.
New York Toronto London Auckland Sydney

ISBN 0-590-41550-6

12 11 10 9 8 7 6 5 4 3 2 1   9/8 0 1 2 3 4/9

Printed in the U.S.A.   01

First Scholastic printing, June 1989

Chapter 1

Sixteen . . .

Carrie Cates was trying to write a song about turning sixteen. She thrummed her nylon-string guitar, moved the capo up one more fret, hummed an aimless tune, and then stared through her bedroom window at the sunny backyard. Not a scrap of an idea would come to her.

Her birthday was in eighteen days, four hours, and twelve minutes. When she thought about it logically, she knew that sixteen might arrive as quietly as a good night's sleep. Nothing magical would happen. Nothing mysterious or undocumented. Her hair would still be the color of manila folders left out in the sun. Her eyes would still be blue, her legs long. There would still be that little gap between her two front teeth that made her self-conscious when she smiled. Overnight Carrie would not master algebra. Nor would a birthday enable her to hit a high "C" or think up three words that rhymed perfectly with "intense." It didn't even mean that she would conquer the Los Angeles freeways or pass her driver's license test.

So why make a big deal about turning sixteen? Why even try to write a song about it?

Stan was the big deal about turning sixteen . . . Carrie's new stepfather, Stan. Stan had marked off Carrie's life the way some historians marked off civilizations. In history there was B.C. and A.D. and in Carrie's life there was P.S. and A.S. . . . pre-sixteen and after sixteen. Right now Carrie was still pre-sixteen, and consequently Stan forbade heavy metal music, one-on-one dating, staying out after 10:30, R-rated movies, hair dye, pierced ears, cigarettes, mopeds, and high heels. Stan had two grown-up kids from his first marriage, so he was convinced he knew everything about raising teenagers. In the ten months that he'd been married to Carrie's mother, he'd taken over Carrie's life like some kind of dictator. He'd invented so many rules and regulations that Carrie referred to their new house as "the don't-do-anything zone."

"I love you as if you were my real daughter," Stan would say, "and I want us to respect one another. But if you want to do that and live in my house, you're going to have to wait until you're at least sixteen."

That was the kind of statement that made Carrie want to scream, to shout, to take Stan by the roots of his graying hair and fling him around the cul-de-sac. But of course she couldn't do that, so instead she and Stan did what they were doing right now — they engaged in cold war.

"Carrie, are you in there?"

It was Stan's voice at her bedroom door. He sounded like a mixture of Bob Newhart and General Patton. Carrie didn't answer, hoping that if she ignored him and waited long enough, he would simply go away. He didn't. Instead he knocked. And knocked again.

Her mother chimed in. "Carrie, can we talk to you?"

"I'm busy." Carrie set her guitar in its case and instead plunked a tape into her blaster. David Bowie blasted. Trying to get some inspiration from the beat, she sat at her desk, drummed the top, and stared at her bulletin board. Pinned up were scraps of music paper, sheet music, record jackets, and her program from the Hollywood production of Les Misérables. A row of photos was across the middle of the board. Carrie focused on the photo-booth shots of her two best friends, Zane and Mary Beth. At Sherman High the three of them were called the Triumphant Trio. Of course, they were also called the Terrible Trio, the Tacky Trio, and the Tumultuous Trio. In the photo Zane was making a wild face, her one earring dangling, the pink streak gleaming in her long, dark hair. Mary Beth was holding two fingers behind Zane's head, giggling and looking about ten years old. If only Zane and M.B. were with Carrie right now. Zane would have the perfect flip comeback to drive Stan crazy. Or Mary Beth would react with such innocence and regret that Stan would melt and forget this whole thing.

"Carrie, I want to talk about our argument this morning. I don't like leaving things this way."

"Stan, I told you," Carrie called back, "I'm doing something important."

"Carrie, can you turn that music down?"

"I can't hear you."

"CARRIE!"

The door swept open and Stan walked in. Even though it was Saturday, he was wearing a starched white shirt with his Bermuda shorts. His legs were unbelievably white. Stan was a dermatologist and believed that suntans were bad for peoples' health.

"We need to talk, Carrie," he said. He marched over and turned off the blaster. It became so quiet that Carrie could hear the air conditioner hum. "Don't shut me out."

Carrie softened when she noticed the pleading expression on Stan's face. But then she saw her mother leaning in the doorway. Her mom was as blonde and leggy as Carrie and wore the same tight-lipped expression when she got angry. Carrie couldn't help wondering why, after being divorced for thirteen years, her mother had suddenly decided on pale, uptight Stan. At least she could have waited one more year to marry him. At least she could have waited until after Carrie turned sixteen.

"Maybe *you* need to talk," Carrie answered. "I don't. I didn't ask you to be my stepfather."

"I never said you did."

Carrie looked back at her bulletin board. Besides photos of Zane and Mary Beth, there was one other photo that made Carrie feel hopeful and free. Her father. Her *real* father. Carrie barely knew him. But since Stan had entered the picture, she'd realized that he was just what was missing from her life. With his handlebar mustache and worn blue jeans he looked more like a cowboy or a rafting guide than a father. He lived alone in Northern California and was an incredibly popular teacher at Mission College. In eight days Carrie was going up to visit him. Eight endless June vacation days. She touched his picture. When she finally shifted to face Stan and her mom, she noticed that both of them were frowning.

"You'll see him soon enough," Stan grumbled. He sounded hurt.

"Not soon enough for me."

"Don't blame me for that," Stan reminded her. "I helped arrange for you to spend more time with him this summer."

"I know," Carrie had to admit.

This was the only area where Stan's "sixteen" rules had worked in Carrie's favor. Stan had wanted Carrie to take his last name after her birthday. He said that since she didn't see her real father all that much she might as well call herself Carrie Morrison, after him. "No way!" Carrie had screamed, and it turned into one of their huge fights. Somehow it had ended with Stan conceding that Carrie should spend more time with her real father. Usually she only saw her dad over Christmas and spring break. He was always so busy, and her mother did everything to keep the visits few and far between. This would be the first summer she had visited him since she was ten years old.

"I still don't know why you want to go up there," her mom said. "That summer cabin of his is so run-down."

"It is not," Carrie shot back, even though she barely remembered what the cabin looked like. "You know, every place doesn't have to be like this stuffy house."

Her mom rolled her eyes. She and Carrie's father had one of those "nothing my ex does is right" relationships. Carrie figured there were two sides to every divorce, and she couldn't understand how her mom could prefer Stan to Daniel Cates. There was simply no contest. It was like her high school principal versus Tom Selleck.

But right now Stan was on the attack. He dragged Carrie's pink corduroy pillow chair from where it sat crumpled next to the window seat. Pulling it close, he plopped down, making his white knees stick up under his chin. Carrie's mother didn't move from the doorway.

"Carrie," he said in a controlled voice, "I know you're angry and that you thought I was being unfair — "

"Stan, forget it. I know what you think. I can't do anything until I'm sixteen. And when I turn sixteen you'll tell me I have to wait until I'm twenty-one."

"Carrie," her mother ordered, "let Stan talk."

Carrie huffed. This morning's argument had started because she wanted to go to the beach. They lived in "the Valley," the smoggy, sterile suburbs of L.A. Carrie and her mom had always lived here, but at least they used to live closer to Ventura Boulevard, so that Carrie could walk to the tennis courts or to meet Zane and Mary Beth at the Taco Bell. But Stan's house was four miles up in the hills, in a subdivision called Valencia Overlook Estates. About the only places within walking distance were the San Diego Freeway and the guardhouse that announced the entrance to the neighborhood.

As far as Carrie was concerned, the best thing about Southern California summers was the beach. Other than that they were mostly about smog, stale air-conditioned air, and over-chlorinated swimming pools. But Santa Monica Beach was a half hour away — by freeway. Since Zane and Mary Beth weren't sixteen yet, either, they were the Trapped Trio. Not a license among them. The only ride they'd been able to find that morning was with some unnamed friend of Zane's brother's. Naturally, Stan had forbidden it. "Talk," Carrie said finally.

"Thank you. Now. You know that we have rules about who you get in a car with. You know that."

Carrie hated Stan's royal "we." "And I told you that Zane's brother's friend is a good driver."

"How do you know?"

"I know."

"How?"

"I just know. I didn't give him a test or anything."

"Carrie, you admitted that you've never met him."

"So?"

"So, you don't know what kind of car he's driving. You don't know which beach he's going to or when he's coming back. What if there's an undertow? What if one of you got hurt? You don't even know which of Zane's brothers he's friends with!"

"He's just giving us a ride, Stan! Mary Beth's mother said it was okay."

"I doubt that," her mother piped up again. "I tried to call her and she wasn't home. Mary Beth does whatever you and Zane tell her to do."

"Zane's parents don't mind."

"Zane's parents don't mind much of anything. Besides, if Zane's parents let her jump off a cliff, would you jump, too?"

Carrie could have predicted that one. "What am I supposed to do, Mom?" she finally exploded. "Sit in my room all the time? I can't get anything done here!"

"Don't be so dramatic."

"I'm not being dramatic!" Carrie took a deep breath. It drove her crazy when Stan accused her of overacting. If only Stan knew how she *really* felt. Her insides had begun crashing like a wave on Venice Pier.

"I don't know why you need to go to the beach anyway," Stan said. "You can swim here."

Carrie stared out her window, squinting from the glare that bounced off their backyard swimming pool. She took in the white patio and the potted cactus plants, the sprinklers waving across the orange trees, and the bright green grass. Stan probably thought she wanted to go to the beach to get a perfect tan or flirt with the surfers. That wasn't it at all. For Carrie, the roar of the waves inspired bass lines. The squawking of the gulls gave her ideas for melodies. And the crowded, constantly changing scene helped her think up lyrics and rhymes. She wanted experience, something to write about. The most interesting thing around Stan's house was the automatic pool sweep.

"I feel cooped up here," Carrie tried to explain. "It's boring."

"I told you to sign up for that Italian class," Stan came back. "But you wanted to go away instead." He glanced at her mother as if to repeat, "I told her so."

Stan would never understand. He certainly didn't understand her music, and as far as Carrie was concerned, that meant he didn't understand anything about her. He'd suggested that she spend this summer playing soccer or being a camp counselor. When she'd argued that her foremost interest was in writing songs, he'd suggested that she take Italian and study opera. Then he told her that her Walkman was damaging her hearing and ordered her to turn down the music she played in her room.

"Besides," Carrie said, eager to change the

subject, "I feel deserted up here. Zane and Mary Beth live all the way on the other side of the Boulevard."

Her mother had stepped into the bedroom. She stood behind Stan and put her hands on his shoulders. "It's only for another week. Then you'll be up at Watson River with your father. Zane and Mary Beth will be with you. It's not as if you're not going to see them all summer."

"You wouldn't care if I didn't see them all summer."

"Carrie."

"It's true." Stan wouldn't have dreamt of inviting Zane and M.B. on a vacation with him, the way her real father had. As soon as the plans for this summer had been settled, her dad had called back to say, "Bring your two best friends. I don't want you to miss them." All Stan ever said about Zane and M.B. was that Zane was too wild, and that Mary Beth never stood up for herself.

"Carrie," Stan sighed, putting his face in his hands. "I just don't know what you want."

Carrie didn't know how Stan could be so dense. She lived in the land of freeways, drive-in banks, and block-long car washes, yet she was stranded. She wanted to be special, gifted, while he wanted her to be ordinary and safe. She yearned for freedom and independence, and all anyone told her was, "Wait until you turn sixteen!"

"I want my life to change," she suddenly told them. "Mom, you think your life is all fixed now.

But I want something more than just living in a nicer house. I want — "

Her mother's face went red. "Carrie, I didn't marry Stan just to live in a nice house."

"It's okay," Stan interrupted, although it was obvious that he was losing his temper, too. His brow was creased and his hands were beginning to shake. "Carrie, don't act like a brat."

"I'm not a brat!"

"Carrie, just be quiet," her mother insisted.

"Why should I be quiet? He's the one who called me a brat!"

Her mother put her face in her hands. "Stop this, both of you!"

They stopped and stared at the carpet. There was just the sound of the dishwasher changing cycles in the kitchen and the bird of paradise bush brushing against the side of the house.

"Carrie, I can't take much more of this," Stan said after the pause.

"You're not the only one." Carrie looked around her bedroom. The whole place was closing in on her. The shag carpet and the light gray walls. The alarm clock. The window shades that were the color of sidewalks. The desk organizer Stan had given her, filled to the brim with erasers and stamps and paper clips. She wanted to break away from everything so sterile and so dull. She wanted something else in her life besides the smoggy Valley, Stan and her mother, and always thinking about turning sixteen.

Stan had stood up and was shaking his head.

"I don't know why you make me so mad."

"You make me just as mad, Stan."

"Can't you two just talk to one another calmly?" her mother pleaded.

"It's not my fault. Maybe we just weren't meant to live in the same house." Suddenly Carrie's brain felt electrified, and out of that brightness came a strange clarity, as clear as the water in the pool. "You're always telling me that things will change when I turn sixteen. Well, maybe that's true," she blurted. "Maybe they will *really* change. Maybe on my birthday, when I'm up with my dad, I should think about moving up with him. For good. Maybe I should talk to him about it."

"What?" her mother gasped.

"Oh, Carrie," sighed Stan. "Don't be ridiculous."

"I should!" Carrie continued, not quite believing what she'd said. When Stan and her mother had married, Carrie had brought up the possibility of living with her father. The subject had quickly been dropped. There were so many reasons why it didn't seem realistic. Her dad had been alone since she was three. During the school year he lived in a small apartment in San Francisco. Summers were spent at the river cabin where Carrie was going to visit him. He traveled. He had a million friends. He drove an old truck, kept a scruffy dog, and probably didn't eat balanced meals or pick up his clothes.

"Oh, Carrie, don't be so foolish."

Carrie ignored their shocked reaction. She had

this fabulous spark inside, the one she got when she wrote a tight lyric or heard a great new song. "I should! You always said that when I finally turn sixteen, I can decide things for myself. Well, maybe that's what I'll decide. Maybe I'll move up with him next fall and then we'll never have to argue again!" Carrie's voice echoed and finally faded away. For a long time the three of them stood there, staring at the carpet, not saying anything.

"What makes you think — " her mother started to say.

Stan held up a pale hand. "Let's let this rest for a while." He looked fed up now. Tired. He started out and Carrie's mom slowly followed.

"I'm serious," Carrie said as Stan and her mother reached the doorway.

Stan turned back. "I'm sure you are."

The door closed.

Carrie leaned back in her deck chair. Her heart was slowing down. The urgency and frustration she'd felt with Stan was starting to ease, melting into something much more fluid and easy.

"Hi, Dad," she whispered, gazing at her father's rugged and handsome face. She knew so little about him, and yet she knew so much. He'd left early in her life, and yet she'd always felt that he was waiting to come back. He seemed to be smiling at her. A special smile. She tried to find a resemblance between her wistful, delicate features and his open, adventuresome face. He was much darker than she. But the dreamy blue eyes were the same. As was the space between the two front teeth, although his gap looked wider since he grinned so much more broadly.

Carrie wondered what it really would be like to live with her father. In her daydreams she imagined perpetual summer. Not closed-in Los Angeles summer, but river summer. Wild blackberries. Bare feet. Old flannel sleeping bags that smelled like trees. The more she thought about what she'd so unthinkingly blurted to Stan and her mother, the more it made sense to her. Soon she would be sixteen, and sixteen was the perfect age to start life all over again.

Chapter 2

Mary Beth Tamarack had been on the phone all day. Her mother always said that she, Zane, and Carrie needed three-way telephones. Once they'd spent an entire afternoon trying to call each other at exactly the same moment to see if they could create a triple connection. But it didn't work, so they continued their endless pattern of "I'll tell Carrie," or "you call Zane," or "call me back after you talk to Carrie," or "have Zane call me and let me know where things stand."

"How about if we meet tonight at the Taco Bell," Mary Beth was telling Carrie this time. She was curled up in her mom's overstuffed chair, lifting her bare shoulder to relieve the crimp at the back of her neck. She'd been listening to Carrie for forty-five minutes. This was the twelfth call over the last few days. Mary Beth was a very good listener.

"I won't be able to get down to the Boulevard later," Carrie complained. "Stan and my mom are leaving now to go to some party. They won't be back until late. And I'm not allowed to even ride my bike after dark. Not before I'm . . ."

"SIXTEEN," they both said at the same time.

"What am I going to do?"

"Wait," Mary Beth told her. She bit her lip and thought. Mary Beth often thought the hardest when she was trying to help her friends do what they wanted to do. "Let me ask my mom. Maybe she'll pick you up and drive you down to the Taco Bell."

"Really? But she'd have to drive all the way up here just to take me back down."

"Let me ask. You know how my mom likes anything that gets me out of the condo. Even if it *is* just to meet you two goons."

"Thanks."

Mary Beth leaned back and called to the kitchen. She had to call three times before her mom heard her, since her voice was so breathy and soft. Finally her mom answered.

"She said okay," Mary Beth came back, a little surprised. "She'll drive you and then pick us all up later."

"M.B., you're the best," Carrie cried. "What would Zane and I do without you?"

"I don't know," M.B. replied. "You'd be the same, I guess."

"M.B.! We would not."

Mary Beth smiled. "Maybe you would miss me. I think Zane would, anyway."

"We both would. M.B., you're great. See you later."

"Okay. 'Bye."

After hanging up, Mary Beth curled her feet under her thighs, almost folding herself in half. Her peach-colored hair, which framed her face in a loose, boyish cut, flopped over her eyes. She was so slim-shouldered and lanky that she looked a lot younger than almost sixteen. She sure felt a lot younger than almost sixteen. Carrie made sixteen sound like this mystical experience that would turn Mary Beth into the head of the ski club, a varsity cheerleader, or a smokey-voiced vixen who drove boys wild. M.B. wished for things like that before she hugged her stuffed panda and fell asleep. But she knew that she would wake up the same freckle-faced, soft-spoken, nearly invisible M.B.

"Is Carrie feeling better?" Mary Beth's mom called from the kitchen.

"I think so," Mary Beth answered. "I guess she had another fight with Stan. She said thanks for offering to drive her tonight."

"Of course. I don't want her to stay home and stew, especially if she and Stan had some kind of scene."

Mary Beth agreed. She hated scenes. She'd been famous in grade school as the girl who burst into tears if a teacher looked at her the wrong way. But Carrie was so intense that she had to brood and struggle over everything. And Zane . . . well, Zane got bored when life was calm and stirred things up just for the fun of it. Like the time in middle school when the three of them had stayed after in Mr. Podesker's science lab. Zane decided to liberate the white mice. Then Carrie

17

worried that the mice would starve, so she put out piles of food in every corner. And Mary Beth stood watch at the door the whole time, terrified that they were going to get caught and kicked out of school for the rest of their lives.

That was just how Mary Beth was feeling now. Well, maybe not terrified. But certainly nervous. There was a kind of uneasy feeling in the pit of her stomach, as if she'd just eaten straw or peanut shells. It was a feeling that said that her life was lurching off in a direction she wasn't sure she really wanted to go.

"M.B., I'll be in in a minute," her mother called again. "I want to talk to you."

"About what?"

"About your trip up to Watson River to visit Carrie's father."

"Oh."

Mary Beth picked up the paperback she'd been reading before Carrie'd called and tried to distract herself. Usually it worked, since she was a voracious reader. When she was little she'd been known to cross busy streets while holding a book in front of her face. She could get equally absorbed in old movies, video games, Saturday morning cartoons, and experiments with her chemistry set. And yet, tonight nothing would distract her. Not even Ray Bradbury stories or Garfield or litmus paper that turned twelve shades of blue.

So she burrowed into her chair and examined the condominium she shared with her mother. She liked the safe darkness of the study. The tall old lamp from her mother's insurance office. The dark shutters that kept out the harsh California light and constant noise of the Valley traffic. She and her mother had lived in this building since her dad had died, when Mary Beth was a baby. Mary Beth was used to it. In a way it bugged her that she liked such cozy, domestic stuff. She wouldn't have minded her life being more like the books she read and the movies she rented. But when it really came down to actually doing something, like this river trip, she just got that scratchy feeling.

"I want to make sure you have everything you'll need for the trip," her mom called over the rumble of the Cuisinart. "We need to find out how cold it gets up at the river, things like that. Maybe you should call Carrie again and ask her."

Mary Beth sunk deeper. The more Carrie talked about how she couldn't wait to see her father, the stronger that weird feeling became. The more Zane cheered about the adventures they were going to have, the more Mary Beth worried. Mary Beth couldn't have stood the idea of Carrie and Zane taking off to some exotic place without her. And yet, she knew what kind of crazy situations they got into just going to the Little League field or the drug store. Zane always wanted to sneak into the boys' dugout or pretend to the store clerk that she didn't speak English. And Carrie drifted off to listen to the leaves rustle or argue with some stranger about why a certain song wasn't good and how she'd make it better.

Maybe that was why Mary Beth had to go to the river with them, in spite of her fears that she might get stomach cramps or be stung by a bee. Maybe if it weren't for her, Carrie would get so intense and distracted that she would drift off the planet. And Zane would do something so nutty that she would wind up in juvenile hall.

"Now," her mom said, appearing at the door with a pad and pencil in hand. She was as freckled as her daughter, but heftier and more put together. She still wore her office skirt and bow tie, although the cuffs of her blouse were rolled up. A yellow Post-it was stuck to her sleeve. She sat on the arm of the chair and read the list she'd made for herself. "Do you need hiking boots?"

"Hiking boots? I don't think so."

"Wool socks?"

"I'm not sure."

"How about a canteen, M.B.?"

"Mom, it's not Outward Bound or anything."

As usual, her mom picked up on her fear right away. "Mary Beth, what are you worried about? You should be excited about going on a vacation with your friends."

"I am. Sort of."

"You're almost sixteen."

"I know."

"You're old enough to really enjoy an opportunity like this."

If Carrie thought her problems were going to be solved by turning sixteen, Mary Beth feared the opposite. When her mom referred to sixteen, the reference was to getting tough with the world. Facing challenges. Becoming serious about college, opening a bank account, looking for a part-time job. Meanwhile, Mary Beth still got homesick when she spent the night at Carrie's. She cried when she watched *Bambi*. She had a hard time returning a pair of jeans, talking to receptionists, or applying for a library card.

"Are you really having second thoughts? Carrie and Zane are counting on you."

"I know." Mary Beth didn't want to let her friends down. Zane and Carrie were the only reasons Mary Beth wasn't a complete washout. At Sherman High she was known as Zane's best friend, Carrie Cates's close buddy. People invited her to parties because they wanted Zane to liven things up. They asked her opinions of concerts and rock stars because they knew she was close to Carrie. If Mary Beth wasn't part of their trio she'd probably be known as the Freckled Black Hole.

"I bet you three have a wonderful time," Mrs. Tamarack said pointedly, as if she could read Mary Beth's mind. "M.B., sometimes you just have to take a chance. Do things and have new experiences. You can't spend your whole life sitting home and reading books. The summer before you turn sixteen should be the best summer of your life."

"It should?"

"Don't you think so?"

"I guess," Mary Beth sighed, even though she wasn't at all convinced. She wanted to say, "No, I'm worried that this summer will be a totally weird disaster. I'm worried that the summer before I turn sixteen will be the worst summer of my life." But she didn't say a word. Certainly not "no." She didn't say no very often. Maybe that was another thing she'd have to do when she finally turned sixteen.

That night Zane Mazerski sat with Carrie and Mary Beth outside the Taco Bell on Ventura Boulevard. Her silver shoes tapped the gum-dotted concrete. Her painted fingernails clacked happily on the hard tabletop.

"So did Stan flip out again today?" Zane wondered.

"Sort of," Carrie answered. "Minor flip-out over what kind of bathing suit I could buy for the river. On a scale of ten, I'd say it was only a three."

"I still can't believe you said you wanted to move up with your father," groaned Mary Beth. "I can't believe you said that to Stan!"

Carrie smiled. "Me, neither. I hadn't really thought about it until it came flying out of my mouth."

"That's the best way to think about things," Zane grinned.

"Or not think about them," reminded M. B.

Zane began to giggle. A blush spread across her chest, up her shoulders, into her neck until it crossed her face. Fifteenth summer was the best summer yet. Zane wouldn't turn sixteen until next January, but she didn't mind waiting. To her, summer was no time to worry about what was going to happen, or what had been. The summer before turning sixteen should be like an L.A. freeway, Zane decided. Fast. Crowded. Concentrated. All they needed to do was close their eyes, jump into a lane, and find out where it was going to take them.

Zane leaned over the table, demanding her friends' attention. "Let's forget about Stan and think happier thoughts. Okay. We'll be there soon. Picture it. Zoom, zoom. The plane to San Fran." She picked up a taco shell and mimed a banking airplane. "Then, *wa-hoo*. Meeting Carrie's real dad. Ahhhhh!" She demonstrated a gushy reunion between the salsa cup and a tortilla chip. "Then, driving over to the river." Zane took the cardboard container and marched it across the table. "Watson River, get ready!"

Mary Beth and Carrie were laughing. That was Zane's job in this three-way friendship. Mary Beth was the brake to slow Zane down and keep her from crashing. Carrie was the steering wheel to lead her to new and interesting places. And Zane was the fuel. She could make them take off and sometimes almost explode. Deciding that they weren't laughing hard enough, Zane made her famous Godzilla lips — a face in which she tried to turn all her features upside down. Soon they were spitting ice and soda over the tabletop.

"Stop!"

"Zane, don't do that. I'm drooling."

"I'll never stop," Zane bragged. "And M.B., you always drool."

"I do not!"

They sat back, smiling at one another and picking at stray pieces of lettuce and cheese. The cars flashed by on the Boulevard and the smell of onions and smog hung thick in the warm air.

Zane twirled her single earring. Her dark hair fell into waves down past her shoulders, and the pink streak glistened under the Taco Bell floodlights. "I'm so glad we decided to meet here tonight. I was going crazy at home."

"Zane, you're always crazy."

"True." Zane pulled her checkered-framed sunglasses down until they rested on the tip of her nose. "Everyone knows that except my family. My brothers think I'm a twerp and refuse to drive me to the beach ever again. And when I tried to complain to my parents, they acted like they didn't even remember who I was."

"Really?"

"Really."

Zane was the fifth of seven kids. It seemed as if there was nothing she could do that hadn't been done before. Zane's parents never got very excited over her. Not when she streaked her hair. Not when she got sent home for arranging parties in the school bathroom to smoke clove cigarettes. Not even when she, Carrie, and Mary Beth took the bus to Hollywood and had to hitchhike home.

Mary Beth was blowing into her straw now, making a rumbling, slurpy noise. "How could anyone not remember you, Zane? They might not remember me, but *you* make a lasting impression." Zane made another face. "And your brothers think everyone who's younger than they are is a twerp."

"They just think they're cool because they can drive. Well, we'll show them," Zane bragged. "As soon as we all turn . . ."

No one said it, but at the same time they all flashed sixteen fingers. It was one of those group rituals they did automatically, like the way they all wore the same colors on Fridays, or made sure they had the same gym period and the same lunch every single semester.

Zane nudged Mary Beth. "Thanks. My brothers are bozos." Mary Beth usually said the right thing to make her feel better. "I don't want to drive to the beach with them anyway. People might think we're related."

"I agree," said Carrie.

They assumed a more relaxed posture — Carrie leaning against Mary Beth; Mary Beth affectionately kicking Zane under the table; Zane perking up to see what else was going on and how she could get in on it. Carrie's loose lacy dress blended with Mary Beth's baggy shorts and Zane's chic off-the-shoulder sweatshirt.

"Just think. We'll be out of here in a few more days." Zane grinned. She was looking around the Taco Bell with that mischievous, hungry Zane expression. "I can't wait. But we still have to remember. These are a few precious days of summer vacation that we don't want to waste."

"Easy for you to say."

"It is easy for me to say," Zane responded

suddenly, gasping and clapping her hand over her mouth. She tossed back her long hair and knocked into Carrie with her strong, tanned shoulder. "Like right this very minute. There happens to be a most interesting view. *Ooo*."

Carrie and Mary Beth looked over. Four bulky boys, juniors-to-be probably, in cut-off football jerseys and mud-stained sweats, were walking by. Carrie ignored them because she'd just had some flash of inspiration and was scribbling words down on a Taco Bell napkin. The boys ignored Mary Beth. Zane smiled at them and nudged the other girls. She always liked company for her most outrageous moves. Mary Beth was usually her best audience, and this night was no exception.

"Zane, I think they like you," Mary Beth whispered.

The boys stared at Zane. Boys usually stared at Zane.

"What did I tell you," Zane whispered. "Open your eyes and you will find wonderful things."

"Zane!" Mary Beth blushed and giggled.

"Shhh." Carrie sighed loudly. She was scribbling on her napkin and chewing a hank of hair. Finally she looked up with a pensive, creased expression. "Zane. We don't want them to come over and bug us. Not right now. I just got an idea. What rhymes with river?"

"Quiver."

"Sliver."

"Liver."

"Carrie, don't do that now," Zane decided.

"They're coming over here. Help me!"

Mary Beth hid her face with her hands. "I don't know what to do!"

"Zane. Wait," Carrie warned, "I'm not finished."

"Come on. Don't leave me on my own here." Zane pouted in a vampy, chin-on-bare-shoulder pose. But just as she was about to stand and prop herself against the table, the boys started gesturing football passes and plays. Soon they had forgotten about Zane and taken their burritos to another table. Zane stared after them for a moment, quiet and disappointed.

"They left," Mary Beth couldn't help commenting.

"They weren't that cute anyway," Zane came back. She leaned over the table again. "Okay. So, did you talk to your dad yet?" Zane asked Carrie, desperate to distract her from her writing. "Can he wait for us to come? Did you tell him you might want to move in with him next year?"

"I talked to him," Carrie answered, finally tucking her napkin notes away. The subject of her father was one of the few things that could grab Carrie's full attention. "I haven't told him everything yet. I have to wait and feel it out. But I bet it will be all right."

Mary Beth looked skeptical. "Do you really think Stan would let you? My mother would be so hurt if I wanted to live somewhere else."

"My parents wouldn't mind," Zane chuckled. "One less kid to keep track of." They all laughed.

But when they stopped laughing, they looked at one another more seriously. "We just have to make sure that we still stay friends if you end up moving away," Zane said, her voice bold and husky. "That's the most important thing. Have a good time and stick together. Right?"

Carrie smiled, her blue eyes getting dreamy and the gap between her teeth starting to show. "Yup. Just think. After all, in a few days it will just be us. Us and my father. At Watson River."

Zane laughed loudly and pitched a handful of ice into the air. "That's right. The last summer before we turn sixteen."

"The summer that I actually *turn* sixteen," Carrie reminded her. She looked across the street, although her eyes didn't focus on the bank building or the cars. "I wonder what it will really be like up at the river."

"We'll find out," worried Mary Beth.

"We have to make this summer last," vowed Zane.

"The summer when everything turns around."

They stuck their hands across the formica tabletop. Zane's fingers — each nail polished a different color — touched Carrie's wrists, which fluttered with thin silver chains, which in turn embraced Mary Beth's freckled fingers. Carrie squeezed her eyes closed. Mary Beth chewed her lip. And Zane laughed softly with the delicious thought that they would soon be on their way.

Chapter 3

"Hey, Phil, where's that sack of homemade taffy?"

Phillip Davison stretched that one inch further — the one inch he knew he probably shouldn't have — and reached to the very highest shelf from the top rung of the creaky wooden ladder. He swayed and swung. He was a human pendulum listing back and forth between boxes of old-fashioned ice cream cones and homemade Watson River Taffy.

"Gotcha," Phillip said as he clenched his fingers around the bag and then yanked it clear from the shelf. The ladder teetered for a moment and Phillip felt like a bug on a car antenna; then the motion slowed and he could laugh. He'd done it. He'd pulled the authentic, old-style taffy from the jaws of disaster. Now he could take the twisted pieces of candy out to the front counter of his family's shop.

"Come on, ladder," Phillip prayed. "Don't fail me now."

He skipped down the wooden rungs. The ladder creaked and groaned as if it were tired. Why shouldn't it be? Like most of the businesses in the tiny town of Watson River, the ice cream shop had been there for a long time. Phillip's grandfather had actually founded the Watson River Ice Creamery and Soda Bar in 1927. It was now called The Sweet Shoppe, but that was about the only thing that had changed. The green swivel stools still stood at the counter. The round glass display jars still held gumballs and licorice. There was still a shelf of original Coca-Cola glasses and a clock that advertised "Watson River Block Ice — Delivery Always Free."

"Phil, boy," his father called out. "You still alive?"

"Barely," Phillip answered, as he emerged from the back room and out into the soda bar. The ceiling fan swatted at the warm summer air circulating above the long freezer holding container after container of homemade ice cream. Phillip often thought of the entire parlor as a miniature weather system, some parts being hot and sticky, and other parts blowy and ice cold. But then Phillip's true love was the outdoors, and whenever he got the chance to compare anything to the wind or the trees or the river, he did it, even if it were only in his head. He dumped the taffy into a display jar and then started setting up a series of trays in front of the ice cream freezer. "Toppings?" he asked.

"Toppings," his dad responded.

Phillip took a knife, dumped a tray of fresh

roasted walnuts onto the counter, and began chopping them up. His father trotted to the back room, just as busy. They had to be. Phillip could tell that the summer crowd was coming. He could already smell that combination of dry heat, gasoline, and churned-up-gravel. Volvos and BMW's were replacing the old trucks and Jeeps that usually cruised Main Street. The bakery was staying open later and the market was starting to stock its shelves with fancy mustards and imported wines. All the shops were gearing up. Everyone said that this summer was going to be better than last summer, which had been better than any summer before.

Better? Phillip sometimes had to wonder if busier really did mean better. He'd lived in this tiny tourist town all his life. All sixteen years. He'd seen the cycle June after June as Watson River went from a rainy backwoods to a loud, crowded beach party. He was used to the pattern, but lately he was starting to worry. The summer people were changing. When he was younger, they had mostly been families, or people who owned run-down cabins and stayed for the whole season. Now they were more likely to be frat brats and thoughtless Marin County yuppies, renting the newer cabins by the weekend and leaving their trash behind for the next renter to clean up.

Not that Phillip didn't appreciate the tourist business. He had to. His family lived off it. Phillip wouldn't have minded if all of Northern California visited the river. The only thing that worried him was the way the town and river were starting to show wear and tear. Animals had died from eating styrofoam and pop tabs from aluminum cans. Campfires were left smoldering. For him the topper had come when they decided to build a McDonald's just off the highway exit, though the town had fought it. The style was going to be a combination of wild west and San Francisco fern bar. But as far as Phillip was concerned, it was the final sign that things had gone too far.

Looking up through the front window, he could see Watson River. The stillness of the water and the sheer, deep blueness moved him. He'd swum, scuba dived, fished, and boated in that river. He knew every inch of it. He loved and respected it. That was why when he looked at the river again he flinched. A motor boat, bright blue and at least twenty feet long, was speeding around Mueller's Bend. The river went messy and white. Phillip heard a violent yelp from the driver as the water sprayed and the boat thumped past.

"Yes," Phillip warned himself. "The summer people are definitely on their way."

"What did you say, Phil?" his father called.

"I said, what's the speed limit around the bend? I thought that was still a swimming area."

"Don't worry about it, Phil. No one swims there anyway. Don't worry about it."

The radio flicked on in the back room and Phillip knew that meant that his father didn't want to talk about speed limits and Mueller's Bend. Phillip went back to his chopping. Like a lot of the business people in town, Phillip's father didn't question the flush of tourist trade. This summer Phillip had been recommended for a workshop in San Jose. It was for gifted juniors interested in the environment. Phillip had wanted to go. *Badly.* He'd argued that Watson River needed to protect itself. He needed to get out of this tiny town and learn about the world, learn how to deal with these pushy, moneyed visitors who came every summer in increasing numbers. But his parents said no. He had to work the ice cream counter. What mattered to them was the business they could do over the summer season and what they could save to make it through the wet, quiet winter months.

So Phillip was stuck. He'd watch the summer unfold as it always had. There would be blackberry shakes, a few stolen hours in his rowboat, and pick-up baseball games with his friends from Watson High. There would be the Fourth of July dance at the roller rink next door. The rich summer kids would come, filled with disdain for a mere local like him. The regulars, like that San Francisco teacher, Mr. Cates, would complain about how the town was changing. But no one would do anything about it. Not even Phillip. He would pull a paper soda-jerk hat down over his curly dark hair and over his brows, and accept the fact that his sixteenth Watson River summer had arrived.

"DADDDDYYYYYYYYYYY!!!!"
Seventy miles south of Watson River, at San

Francisco International airport, Carrie was finally running down the corridor. Her suede boots flew. Lace-trimmed skirts billowed. Her guitar case thumped against her legs. Mary Beth was way behind and even Zane couldn't keep up. Carrie had spotted her father through the glass double doors. But there could have been a brick wall between them and she still would have known that he was there.

"I'M HEERE! I'M FINALLY HERE!!!"

She dodged a baby stroller and a pair of old ladies as if she were a running back. Setting down her guitar case, she threw herself into his arms. Her father swept her up, his mustache tickling her cheek and his hearty laugh bouncing in her ear. He smelled of tobacco and denim and friendly dog. And he kept laughing as he hugged her and twirled her so exuberantly that she thought she would knock down half of San Francisco.

"Oh, Daddy. I'm so glad to see you."

"I know, kid."

"I've missed you so much. I have so much to tell you."

"You can tell me anything."

"About Stan and Mom and me and turning sixteen and oh, Daddy. I love you. Oh. Everything's going to be okay now."

"I love you, too, kid. Let me look at you." Daniel Cates put Carrie down.

Carrie looked at him instead. He was as handsome as she remembered. His jeans were baggy and so worn they were split at the knees. He wore a Mission College sweatshirt and suspenders. His hair was shaggy long, peppered with gray from his temples to his ears. A bandana headband divided his lined forehead from his bright eyes and youthful smile. Suddenly, he clapped his hands and then lunged at her. Carrie crouched and they went into a mock boxing match, which ended with another bear hug. She felt as light and happy as a helium balloon.

By that time Zane and Mary Beth had caught up. Zane was greedily taking in every male, every suitcase, every advertisement, window, and video screen. She was grinning and bouncing on the heels of her sandals, which were patterned like zebra fur.

"These are my two best friends," Carrie announced, stepping away from her father to join M.B. and Zane. "Thanks for inviting them. Summer could never be as good if they weren't here, too."

"I believe that," Carrie's father said, smiling at Zane and Mary Beth.

"Hi, Mr. Cates," Zane said, taking off her sunglasses and sticking them in her mouth. She tossed her streaked hair over her shoulder. Her single earring swung.

Unlike Stan, Carrie's father didn't react at all to Zane's wild appearance. He merely stuck out a hand for a respectful handshake. Then he hesitated before greeting Mary Beth, as if he sensed right away that she didn't want to compete with Zane's boldness.

"You can call me Dan," her father told them both in a gentle voice. "If you want to, that is."

"Great. Thanks. You can still call me Zane."

Mary Beth finally stepped out from behind Zane and blushed. "I'm Mary Beth, Mr. Cates. I mean, um . . . Dan."

"Welcome." He shook Mary Beth's hand, too. She stared at the floor and blushed again. "Welcome to San Francisco. Any friends of Carrie's are friends of mine." The four of them stood there for a moment, not sure what else to say. "How was the flight?"

"Short," Zane answered right away. "I've flown before. Mary Beth got kind of pukey."

"I did not." Mary Beth had two sweaters tied around her waist and a sci-fi novel in her hand. Three carry-on bags were piled next to her feet. Everything was labeled. Even her tennis shoes and her jumper had her name printed on them. She shrugged. "Maybe a little. We dipped about a million feet right before we landed."

"A million, Mary Beth?" Zane and Carrie teased at the same time.

"It was scary! But I guess I didn't have to use the barf bags or anything."

Mr. Cates laughed. "I'm glad to hear that, Mary Beth."

"All that matters is that we're here," Carrie said. The three girls hugged one another. "We made it." Carrie let go of her friends and hugged her father again instead.

"That's right." There was another pause as Mr. Cates and Carrie grinned at each other. Finally, he checked his watch, then scooped up Carrie's guitar and Mary Beth's bags. He announced loudly, over the flight announcements and the rumble of the quick-moving crowd, "Let's not waste time hanging around the airport. There's too much to do at the river. Let's go!"

"Okay!" Zane agreed.

"Okay," Mary Beth mumbled, much less surely.

Mr. Cates led the way to the baggage claim. Zane hurried along, disappearing into every newsstand and café, only to reappear each time with an even bigger grin. Mary Beth followed with a woeful attempt at a smile. And Carrie sailed. That was how she felt. Free. As if she were a box kite or a swallow, floating on a fresh, new breeze.

Carrie was astounded at how quickly her life was being transformed. Just as she'd hoped it would. Only an hour ago she'd been at the Los Angeles airport with Stan hovering. The air had been muggy and smelled of tar. As soon as she'd stepped off the airplane in San Francisco, Carrie had felt the difference. There was a breeziness, a sea-salt feel to the atmosphere here. The light was softer, more pastel. And her father was with her. Her real father. She walked faster to match his pace until he proudly linked her arm with his.

As soon as they arrived at the baggage carousel, their things tumbled down. Once they retrieved their duffels and sleeping bags, time sped up with a rush. They gathered their possessions and rushed out to the parking lot.

"Here we are," Mr. Cates welcomed. His pickup truck was waiting nearby. There was no mistaking it. It was so ancient that it had running boards and fat, round fenders. A golden Labrador sat patiently panting in the back.

"That's Melvin," Mr. Cates told them. Carrie leaned over the wheel to hug the dog. "Mel, say hello to Zane and Beth."

Melvin wore a bandana around his neck that matched Mr. Cates's. He stuck a paw out over the truck's bed for Zane to shake. Mary Beth got up on tiptoes to pet him and he instantly slobbered on her face. Melvin's obvious preference for M.B. seemed to cheer her up a little.

Zane jumped onto the running board. "Dan, can I ride back here with Melvin?"

"If it's okay with Melvin."

"Come on, M.B.," Zane cried, climbing into the bed of the pickup and stacking the bags. "Let's ride in the back. Melvin insists."

Mary Beth's freckled face tensed up again. She looked back and forth from the cab to the bed, as if waiting to be told where to ride. "I think I'd rather ride up front."

"It's up to you, Mary Beth," said Carrie's father.

Carrie quietly slid into the cab. She tried to find the seat belt right away, in the hopes that there would be only one belt and M.B. would have to ride in back. She didn't want to come out and say it, but even though Zane and M.B. were her very best friends, she wanted to be alone with her father. Since she saw him so infrequently, it was like meeting a new person each time. There was so much to catch up on, so much to ask and find out. But luckily, she didn't have to worry about Mary Beth intruding. Zane was pulling her into the truck bed. Mary Beth gave a pleading look to Carrie, but Zane, as usual, got her way.

They took off. After some heavy city traffic, they joined the commuters headed for the Golden Gate Bridge. An aura of calm and peace went over them as they rumbled across it. The water glistened below and the red suspension cables were strung out so gracefully that Carrie wanted to weep with joy. The traffic speeded up again once they crossed the bridge and headed north into the suburbs. They drove for a long time past clumps of white condos and spread-out shopping malls. It was growing cooler and dusk was starting to fall.

"So what's doing at home?" her father said.

Carrie was glad that he'd opened the conversation. It had become so quiet that she was starting to feel as if she were traveling with a stranger or on a first date. "Oh, you know Stan," she told him. "He doesn't take my music seriously. And I can't do anything. He keeps telling me it's because I'm not sixteen."

"I never think about what age you are," her father responded. "To me, a person is a person. Age has nothing to do with it."

"Right!" They were quiet again. After a few minutes, Carrie's exhilaration started to droop. It was true that her father never made a big deal out of her age. He never forgot her birthday completely, but about half the time his presents were a week or so late. "I mean, sixteen is one of the more important birthdays, I know that," she hinted. "But I still don't think that everything should depend on it. It's not like I'm going to turn into a totally different person or anything."

He touched her cheek. "I hope not."

Carrie was starting to worry. She didn't expect a sweet sixteen party. She was even prepared to wait until she got back to the Valley to take her driving test. But she did think that they'd at least do something. "You do remember that my birthday is next week, don't you, Dad?"

He started laughing and nudged her with his elbow. "How could I forget? I've been trying to figure out what to get you. How about a hot air balloon?"

"A what?"

"A lifetime supply of 'E' strings."

"Hmm."

"How about your very own pet llama?"

Pretty soon they both were laughing and remembering the weird presents he'd given her in the past. A bamboo flute. A hundred plastic dinosaurs. A giant book of songs in Spanish. Carrie suddenly realized that her father would never ignore anything as important as this birthday. She felt dumb for ever considering such a thing and decided to change the subject.

"Can I turn on the radio, Dad?"

He nudged her shoulder. "Kid, you don't need to ask. Just turn it on."

Carrie found an oldies station and sat back,

feeling as clear and sparkly as the San Francisco Bay. She hummed along with the music.

"I forgot how pretty your voice is, Carrie," her father said as they left Marin behind. The clusters of new buildings were turning to brown slopes dotted with cattle and scrubby trees. "Sing for me all the way up to the river."

"Do you really want me to?" Stan hated it when she sang along with the radio.

"I want you to."

Carrie sang softly, her voice gaining feeling and expression as the light continued to slip away. Back in L.A., she'd stewed over all the things she needed to talk about when she finally saw her father . . . independence . . . Stan . . . her dreams of being a songwriter or a singer, and her fears that she would never be anything but ordinary. Her fears that her life was dull and stifled and would never, ever change. But now it seemed unnecessary to bring up any of those things. She'd felt her life change the minute she'd seen her dad at the airport. Her father used to say to her that they should live life for the moment. Singing old Beatles songs with the radio was perfect, especially when he added a sweet harmony.

By the time they headed off the freeway and onto a two-lane road, Carrie felt the wonderful music of this whole day. She and her dad simply needed to be in the same space to understand what the other was thinking. Her father knew that sometimes people only needed to sing and drive and smile.

It was dark when they reached Watson River. San Francisco had been mysterious enough, with its steep hills and sunlight the color of sand. But this tiny town seemed even more exotic. Carrie hadn't been here since she was ten, and at night she could only see bits and pieces. Occasional half-lit porches and layers of tall trees. Except for a half-finished McDonald's just off the highway, the whole town looked as if it hadn't changed in sixty years. The street lamps were elaborately etched and curved. The roads were unpaved, except for the one-block downtown, where they passed an old-fashioned market, bakery, post office, tavern, gas station, boat shop, roller rink, and The Sweet Shoppe. They saw the river, with the moon reflecting on the ribbon of water.

Then downtown was behind them. They were crossing a short bridge and heading up a hill. Up more dirt roads and suddenly parking in what seemed like the middle of nowhere.

"This is it," her father announced.

Zane had already jumped out, as had Melvin. Their feet made scratching sounds in the quiet night. Mary Beth rubbed her eyes, looking nervous and confused until Carrie's father noticed her uneasiness and gently helped her climb out of the back of the truck.

They collected their things and Mr. Cates led them with a flashlight. Up hundreds of rickety wooden stairs, bordered on either side by thick brambles that smelled sticky and sweet. Melvin trotted ahead of them, barking, and at last they heard his paws clacking across a wooden floor. The cabin appeared in the moonlight.

Carrie remembered it at once. It was a three-room summer cottage, with a large wraparound deck. Her father disappeared into the large living room. A moment later the lights came on and she saw it more clearly. The simple kitchen. The side bedroom. The porch, where they ate most of their meals and where extra guests slept.

"You girls must be tired," said Carrie's father, tossing his backpack into the living room and then leading the way to the bedroom, where the girls would sleep. There was a maple-framed double bed and a mattress on the floor. The girls dropped their duffels and began to unroll their sleeping bags.

"I guess I am," Carrie heard herself admit. She stood in the doorway with her father, her arm around his waist, his around her shoulder. She wasn't quite ready to let him go.

"Where's the bathroom?" Mary Beth was staring uncertainly around her. Zane was tugging the floor mattress over near the window so she could be the first to see the sun in the morning.

"There *is* a bathroom, isn't there?" M.B. worried.

"Right here." Mr. Cates pointed into the hall, then backed away. "I'll give you girls some privacy." He gave Carrie a quick hug. "Tomorrow I'll show you the places on the river where the other kids hang out. You can figure out what you want to do. Sleep well. I'll be in the living room if you need anything."

" 'Night, Dad."

"Thanks for everything, Dan."

"Good night."

They quickly washed up, set out their sleeping bags, and crawled in. Carrie took in a deep breath of flannel and wood and dust. Through the window she could see the old sofa out on the porch, the thick surrounding trees and the circle of dark, star-filled sky. She heard crickets, Mary Beth tossing next to her, her father padding around in the living room, and the contented beating of her heart.

"*Oooo*," Zane suddenly sang in a scary, ghost-story voice. "Are you really asleep? I'm not."

"Zane, don't," pleaded Mary Beth.

"Let's tell ghost stories."

"Zane, I'm scared enough. Please!"

"Good night, you two," Carrie laughed. It was tempting to stay up late. To chat, or just giggle and try to scare one another. Her father wouldn't stop them, if that's what they really wanted to do. He would be the first to understand their need to make jokes or review all the newness of this wonderful day.

But the chatter didn't last long. They were too tired. Carrie's head felt heavy as a tree trunk. Mary Beth's tossing ceased. Even Zane, who was lying on her back gazing out the window, grew calm and still.

"Good night, M.B."

" 'Night, Zane. 'Night, Carrie."

"See you in the morning."

"We made it."

"We're finally here!"

"Zane, shh. Go to sleep."

Smiling, Carrie set her cheek on the cool pillow and snuggled in the sleeping bag. Melvin could be heard roaming around the porch. Her father was making up the living room sofa. Leaves rustled against the bedroom window. Carrie started to ease into a blurry, contented sleep.

She had made it. She was finally home.

Chapter 4

Morning came. Birds chattered. Melvin barked. The sun was bright and even Mary Beth was too excited to sleep in.

"What are we having for breakfast, Mr. Cates?"

"Snails, Mary Beth."

"Snails. We're going to eat snails!"

"M.B. Not that kind of snails. Dad got them at the bakery. They're great."

"Oh. Sorry. I guess I woke up on the wrong side of the sleeping bag."

Carrie hugged M.B., while Zane made what was supposed to be a snail face, which caused Mary Beth to start laughing and spit orange juice. For a moment all three girls froze. They sat still at the porch picnic table and waited to be told to act their age, to stop being obnoxious, to quit playing with their food. But Dan Cates merely smiled and sipped his coffee. They attacked the pastries.

"These are de*lish*," Zane said. "Thanks, Mr.

Cates. Mmm. Yum." She leaned over the picnic table in her huge leopard print nightshirt, her legs bare except for three ankle bracelets.

"Do you want me to drop you down at the river when you're ready?" Mr. Cates asked, feeding pieces of snail to Melvin.

"Whatever," Carrie replied happily. "Sure."

"Good. You can pack up your stuff and make a day of it. I have some things to do."

Carrie, who was licking frosting from her fingers, looked up quickly, her eyes startled and a little hurt. "What?"

"Just for today," he reassured her. "Some people are in from the city. Besides, I don't want to cramp your style. I thought you might like to explore on your own."

Carrie's concern disappeared. Instead, she beamed at Zane and Mary Beth. "Do what you need to do, Dad. We'll be fine," she assured him.

They wolfed down every last sugary bite, then washed up and collected things to take down to the river. There was an array of fabulous junk stowed in the corners of the cabin and the nooks of the porch. Crossword puzzle books, inner tubes and air mattresses in various states of disrepair, old records, dog toys, beach balls, bluebooks, stacks of mail, tools, clothing belonging to past guests, bags of charcoal and half-complete board games. Mary Beth was particularly fascinated by some picture postcards and a collection of mounted butterflies.

"Let's hurry," Zane urged. She had packed her sunglasses, hair brush, and makeup. She wanted to work on her tan, although she was already the brownest of the three. Carrie's skin was pinky gold, like a nectarine. And Mary Beth was her usual shade of freckled milk.

At last Carrie was ready, too. Her blonde hair hung straight and she wore her dad's sweatshirt, a flowing skirt, and her Walkman. She hugged a writing pad and a sack of plums. Mary Beth was dragging two inner tubes, some books, and what looked like a first aid kit. They ran down the wooden steps to the road, dodging the thickets of blackberries on either side.

All three of them rode in the back of the truck this time, with Melvin accompanying Mr. Cates. They let their hair fly and breathed in delicious tree-flavored wind. Zane stood up after they'd rumbled down about a mile of back road and dipped into downtown. They bumped over the Watson River Bridge and saw the water glimmering under the bright sun.

"Hellloo, Watson River," Zane called out, waving her arms and almost dancing. "Are you ready for us? *Ya-hoooo!*" Mary Beth giggled.

A minute later they pulled into the public parking lot. There were lots of cars, but not many people. Just a few families packing up ice chests and some gray-bearded fishermen.

"Where is everybody?" Zane couldn't help blurting. She'd been ravenous for this new place since she'd popped out of her sleeping bag at dawn. All night she'd dreamed of beaches and boys. But now they were at the river, and the only men in sight were over the age of fifty.

"Over there," Mr. Cates reassured her. He pointed back under the bridge and all three girls craned to look. "There's the main swimming beach."

"Oh." Sure enough, on the other side of the bridge was where the crowd had congregated. There was a lifeguard stand there, a patchwork of umbrellas and towels, and a wading area bordered by ropes and football-shaped buoys. If Zane listened hard enough she could make out the far-off beat of boom boxes.

Mr. Cates helped Carrie out of the truck. Melvin jumped down and Mary Beth slung an inner tube over each arm.

"This area here is for putting boats in," Mr. Cates gestured toward the water. A leg of the parking lot led down to a sloping boat dock. "The parking lot by the lifeguard station is always full."

At that moment there was a roar as another truck barreled past them into the parking lot. Zane stared. It was a long, new Ford with a couple of all-terrain vehicles stacked in back. It pulled a sparkly red motorboat. The truck stopped abruptly, right in the middle of the parking lot, taking up four parking spaces. Then the doors flew open and three boys jumped out. They looked eighteen, maybe nineteen years old. All wore madras shorts and polo shirts, except for the driver, who was tanned and gorgeous, with corn-colored hair and a T-shirt that said COLLEGE OF PACIFIC HEIGHTS.

"Oh, my God," Zane whispered, grabbing

Mary Beth so hard she knew she would leave fingernail dents. "Look!"

Mary Beth glanced over, then blushed. "Zane, they're old."

"Not too old."

"They'll never talk to us."

"Wanna bet?"

Just then one of the boys — not the original driver — hopped back in the truck. The other two walked alongside as the vehicle was eased toward the boat ramp. Zane leapt out of the pickup and went after them. Something had gone off inside her, something that said she was finally at the river and it was time to make things happen. These boys *had* to notice her. It was a feeling she got at home when her mother forgot to pick her up after drawing club meetings, or didn't even notice when she'd pierced only one ear. It gave her the sense that she would explode with impatience and a crazy feeling that she was about to turn into the incredible shrinking girl.

"Zane," Mary Beth called after her in a hushed voice. "Where are you going?"

Zane hesitated for the briefest moment, glancing up at Mr. Cates. No matter how cool he seemed, he was still a father. Even her own parents might actually notice what she was about to do. But Mr. Cates was busy with Carrie, who was clinging to him as he showed her how to get to the other side of the beach. Zane couldn't stop herself, and soon she was galloping down the ramp. Closer and closer to the water. Closer to the dock and the hunky college boys, who were busy unhooking the motorboat.

"Nice boat!" Zane yelled out, squeezing courage from somewhere deep inside her. She breathed secret relief at the strength of her husky voice.

The boys were guiding the boat now, easing it into the river. The blond boy didn't seem to hear her. But his friend turned back to look. He wore the blank expression of an MTV addict. Mirrored sunglasses dangled from a cord around his neck. When he slipped them on, he looked like a robot.

Zane was suddenly filled with shame. Mary Beth was right. These boys were too old. They would never pay attention to a girl who was fifteen and a half. Usually Zane didn't worry about not being sixteen yet, but if these boys had asked her real age, the truth would have stuck in her throat. She cocked a hip and swung back her earring, trying to appear nonchalant. She tried to think of excuses to avoid admitting that the boys had snubbed her. She wished with all her heart that Carrie and Mary Beth had come along. Letting her hair fall over her face, she started back up the boat ramp.

Carrie and Mary Beth met her at the top.

"My dad left," Carrie said, her voice lacking its usual musicality. "He showed me how to get to the main beach. He'll pick us up at four."

Zane had turned back and was staring down after the college boys, her face displaying the same subtle disappointment as Carrie's voice.

"Don't worry about those boys," Mary Beth said, bolstering Zane. "The blond one is the only one who's cute. Besides, boys like that make me nervous."

"I know." Zane relaxed. Mary Beth's bolstering had restored her confidence. "They make me nervous, too." She pretended to faint, then tickled Mary Beth. Carrie started laughing, too. "That's the whole point."

"Zane, you're bad!" giggled Carrie.

"True," Zane bragged, posing with her arms in the air. "Very true."

They would have continued laughing and teasing one another if it hadn't been for a sudden, strong male voice, a voice that came from the opposite direction from the motorboat college boys. All three girls froze to listen.

"That gas tank is leaking," the voice said angrily.

It took Carrie a moment to locate him. Finally she saw a tall boy with dark curly hair wearing tan hiking shorts and a green sweatshirt. He carried a canvas sack and held something that looked like tree branches in one hand.

"Are you talking to me?" asked the college boy with the mirrored glasses.

"Yes. Your boat tank is leaking gasoline into the water."

"What do you care? Who are you?"

"My name is Phillip Davison. I live here."

The college boy laughed, a huge, hearty guffaw. Then he turned to his two friends and pointed. "Wait a minute. I know this guy. He works at that dinky, old ice cream parlor." He turned back to Phillip. "You're the soda jerk. Hey, guys, meet Davison, the jerk."

Zane let out a nervous giggle and Phillip looked up. For a moment he stared at all three girls standing at the top of the boat ramp. Then he shook his head at the college boys and threatened, "Call me whatever you want, just fix your stupid gas tank."

The college boy whipped off his glasses to reveal cold, glinty eyes. "I'll have you know that this boat is brand-new. It cost my friend's father a lot of money. The gas tank does not leak."

"Then what's that dripping out of it?" Phillip argued. "Maple syrup?"

Suddenly Zane had broken away from Carrie and Mary Beth and she was loping down the boat ramp, her hair flying behind her and her zebra sandals slapping the asphalt. "If they say it's a new boat, it's a new boat," she said.

Phillip glared.

Zane looked down at the college boys to see if they'd appreciated her support. The boy with the corn-colored hair smiled. Actually smiled! His two friends were still cool, but at least they were nodding their heads. "And a new boat doesn't leak," Zane added coyly. "Right?"

Phillip glanced back up to where Carrie and Mary Beth still stood. He pushed his dark hair off his forehead and huffed disgustedly. Then he started to walk toward a dirt trail that rimmed the edge of the river. "Fine," he grumbled.

"What's the matter?" the boy with the glasses called after him in a falsetto voice. He put his hands on his hips and swayed in a ridiculous imitation of a woman. "Can't take it when a little girl stands up to you? Go back to your soda jerking. JERK!"

Phillip turned around and glared at them. "Just get it fixed, or I'll report you." He threw his canvas bag over his strong shoulder and strode off.

"Oooo. I'm scared," sang the boy with the mirrored glasses.

"I'm weak in the knees," mimicked his buddy.

"Me, too," the boy with the corn-colored hair joined in.

The boys laughed and patted each others' backs. When Phillip was finally out of sight, they went back to working on their boat and Zane stood for a moment, feeling flat and let down, like all the air had been let out of her. She waited a long time for the boys to notice her again, until she knew she looked stupid standing there alone on the ramp. She realized that Carrie and Mary Beth were already walking across the parking lot and turned away to join them.

That was when the boy with the blond hair finally called up to her. "Hey! You!"

Zane's heart clicked into overdrive. She glanced back over her shoulder. "Me?"

"No, your twin sister."

"Ha, ha."

"What's your name?"

"What's yours?"

"I'm Popeye." The blond put his hand on Mr. MTV's shoulder. "This is Pluto." He pointed to the boy standing in the boat. "And my friend at the wheel is Goofy."

"I could have told you that."

"Thanks for taking our side against that townie. How'd you like a boat ride?"

"Who says I want to ride with you?"

He winked at her, then let his eyes drift from her ankles to her dark eyes and back again. He had a cocky, white, stunning smile. "You're dying to ride in this boat with us."

"Don't you wish!" Zane spun on her zebra sandals and ran up the ramp.

The boy laughed.

Giggling and muttering to herself, Zane bolted back across the asphalt. "Popeye. Give me a break." By the time she reached the upper parking lot she was out of breath and a little lightheaded. She looked around for Carrie and Mary Beth. She saw only the fishermen and lots of empty cars. "Where did everybody go?" she whispered in a small voice.

"ZANE!!! COME ON!!!"

With immense relief, Zane spotted Carrie and M.B., who were waiting for her under the bridge. She threw herself after them. When she caught up she grabbed one of M. B.'s inner tubes, almost tackling her. She told them all about Popeye and Goofy and the red motorboat. Then she tickled Carrie until all three of them were laughing and racing one another over to the main beach.

Chapter 5

"The water looks different
at dusk and at dawn.
One day like a painting,
The next like a song.
When will it happen?
When will it change?
When will I . . .

"Ugh. That's awful," Carrie groaned. She strummed one more chord, then set her guitar on the beach blanket and closed her notebook. "I thought I would write one decent song by the time I turned sixteen. But I won't. Never."

"I liked it," Mary Beth offered. "Play it again."

"It's almost as good as 'La Bamba,'" joked Zane.

They sat on the main beach, after being dropped off for the second day. They were surrounded by couples sampling gourmet picnic hampers, toddlers, dogs, card players, and noisy groups of college kids. It was crowded, although there didn't seem to be many sunbathers near the age of sixteen. Zane was stretched out and oiled with lotion. Mary Beth sat in an inner tube, her pink legs sticking out and kicking. Meanwhile Carrie stood up, pulled on a pair of shorts, and wrapped a lacy scarf around her neck.

"Are you going somewhere?" Zane asked, perking up. "I'm getting minorly hungry."

Mary Beth threw gravel on Zane's stomach. "You should have eaten more of those snails."

"No, I won't think about food." Zane turned over to even her tan and flipped the pages of a magazine. She closed her eyes and licked her lips. "Häagen Dazs. Sara Lee. Pepperidge Farm."

Carrie laughed. "I think I'll take a walk."

"Really? I'll come with you." Mary Beth looked around at the college kids and the couples. "Don't leave me here by myself."

"You and Zane stay here. I won't be long." Carrie squinted at the water. "Look after my guitar. And look after Zane, too, while you're at it."

Zane made a face and sat up. "And look after that red motorboat," she called after Carrie. "I want a full report if you see it."

"Okay."

"Let me know if anything exciting happens!"

Carrie trotted down to the water's edge, then glanced up and down the shore, trying to find the most interesting route. Two days of nonstop Zane and Mary Beth made her crave a few minutes alone. She wanted to absorb new sounds and motions. She was serious about wanting to write one decent song before her birthday. Over the last year, when she got frustrated with a song — when she got frustrated with most anything — she blamed it on Stan. But now she was up here with her father, and she still wasn't satisfied.

She found a trail that led along the edge of the water, between a soggy bank of reeds and a wall of overgrown shrubs. The growth became even denser as she walked away from the beach and toward Mueller's Bend, just like the water ran faster and the sounds of the crowded beach faded away. As much as Carrie wanted to concentrate on the gurgle of the river or the wordplay forming in her head, she kept going back to her father. Was he going to remember her birthday? Or would he be too busy with his errands and his friends? She wanted to know if things were really going to change when she turned sixteen, or if she was just being overdramatic, as Stan would say. And she also wondered whether moving in with her father was a real possibility, or just another figment of her overactive imagination.

Maybe she was being too eager about this whole thing. Too pushy. Her father's style was to wait and see what happened. To take things as they come. To explore. Her life now would be an exploration. A journey to a new world, the unknown land of being independent and nearly sixteen. So she stepped away from the shore and down into the shallow water. It was so fast that she could feel the current's power even though it only came up to her shins. She closed her eyes and listened to the music of the riffles, the snap of the breeze, the beat of a bird flapping its wings overhead.

Then she heard another sound, a sound so soothing and rhythmic that she closed her eyes to listen. Every once in a while it would be punctuated by a bird or a rustle of the reeds. But the sound kept going, like a sheet billowing or a waterfall falling over and over.

She didn't open her eyes again until she realized that the sound had stopped.

"Are you okay?" asked a vaguely familiar male voice.

"What?" Carrie looked around. She knew that she must look like a lunatic, standing in a pool of reeds with her eyes closed, waving her hands and tipping her head from side to side.

"Are you all right?" he repeated.

The voice was coming from the middle of the river and she finally saw him. A dark-haired boy in a row boat. Not an ordinary rowboat, but a boat carved out of pale, glossy wood, trimmed with neat, white paint. And not an ordinary boy, either. A handsome, interesting-looking boy with eyes so green she could tell the color from fifteen feet away. He wore only cut-offs and a diving watch. His chest was slim and brown and he had both arms resting easily over the oars.

"I'm fine." Carrie realized that the rhythmic sound had been his rowing. She felt her feet starting to sink into the wet mud and staggered a little as she tried to take a step back.

"Are you sure?"

"I'm sure."

He picked up his oars and looked behind him, as if he were getting ready to row away again. But then he looked back at Carrie, his green eyes locking onto her. The easy, concerned expression on his face evaporated and his forehead creased with anger. At that moment Carrie recognized him as the boy who'd yelled at the college boys about their leaky fuel tank. And she knew from the look in his green eyes that he'd just recognized her as well.

"You're the one from The Sweet Shoppe," she said, flinging out the first thing that came into her mind.

"Phillip Davison, of the famous Watson River Sweet Shoppe family. That's right."

Carrie shivered from the belligerence in his voice. "I'm Carrie Cates."

"Of the motorboat crowd."

"I just got here," Carrie tried to explain, hoping that he would understand that she didn't even know those college boys. She'd been impressed by Phillip. She wanted him to know that she was on his side. But then she flashed back on Zane. She could hardly pretend that she didn't know Zane. And she didn't know how to explain that Zane was one of those wonderful friends who sometimes did dopey things. "My Dad has a cabin here."

He let the boat drift. One of his hands gently tested the water. "Cates. I think I know him. Your dad's the teacher, right?"

"In San Francisco."

"Where do you live?"

"L.A. Well, the Valley. The suburbs of L.A."

"Same thing."

The belligerence was gone, but he was still keeping his distance. In spite of his coolness, Carrie found herself wishing that she could just sit down and talk to him. She realized that she really needed to discuss this strange, bewildering time she was going through. For some reason Zane and M.B. were too familiar, too old hat, too "Valley" to understand. Carrie needed somebody from the outside, someone who could listen objectively and tell her how this summer would add up.

"That's a pretty boat," she offered.

"It's just a rowboat."

"It's beautiful."

He softened. Something like a smile was taking over his face. "You really think so?" Two dimples pushed their way into his cheeks. "Thanks. I made it."

"You built that boat? All by yourself?"

"My dad and a couple of friends helped me. I like rowing better than power boats." He placed his chin on his fist and sat for a moment, checking out her reaction. "You can hear the world around you when you row." He let his head fall back. "You can smell something besides gasoline, and you never have to worry about knocking somebody else over with your wake." He frowned. "Not that most of the summer people do worry about that."

Carrie started to move forward. She'd temporarily forgotten that she was standing in water and almost stumbled when the river slapped against her knees. Phillip lurched to help her, then sat back when he saw that she was all right. For a moment they stared at each other.

"I know what you mean about hearing the world. I write songs," Carrie explained. "Or at least I try to. And I try to hear things like nobody else in the world hears them. Only there's either too much noise covering things up, or else there's nothing to hear!"

"Not in this river," Phillip came in quickly. "Listen. Just listen. Close your eyes and listen."

For a moment they both did that. Carrie heard his boat gently rocking, a bird scamper through the brush, the wind and the water and her own, low, excited breathing. She didn't know why, but the distance between her and Phillip was being washed away. Sharing this act of listening was sharing something private and important. When she opened her eyes again she saw that Phillip was watching her.

"So that's what you were doing," he grinned.

"What?"

"When I came by. You were listening to the water. I thought maybe you were on drugs or possessed by spirits."

"Thanks a lot."

They laughed. Carrie took another step into deeper water. This time Phillip stuck an oar in the water to try and maneuver his boat closer to where she stood. That was when Carrie heard another sound. This screech was so loud that it hardly demanded careful listening.

"CARRIIEEEEE!!"

"HERE YOU ARE!"

"WE FOUND YOUUUU!"

Carrie turned to see Zane and Mary Beth up on the top of the trail. Zane's fuchsia bathing suit stood out like neon against the woodsy slope. Mary Beth was clutching Carrie's guitar.

"WE'RE HUNGRY. LET'S GET SOME LUNCH!"

"BURRITOS!" screamed Mary Beth.

"McDLT's!" M.B. and Zane yelled at the same time.

Carrie saw Phillip flinch as he looked back and forth from her to Zane. "I guess I, uh, have to go," she said.

Still staring up at Zane, he put the oars back in the water. "I should go, too. I have to be back at work. I'm on my lunch break."

Carrie backed toward the shore. "Of course. Well, maybe I'll see you at the shop. I'll have to stop in and get an ice cream."

"Or maybe I'll run into you in town."

"Or on the beach."

Phillip turned the boat and began to row downstream. "See you."

"I guess."

He turned back and his dimples showed again. " 'Bye. Nice listening with you."

"You, too." Carrie ran up the trail to join Zane and Mary Beth. When she'd almost found them, she stopped to look back. Phillip's boat was gliding down the river, each stroke even and clean. The sun glistened off the white trim and the oars and Phillip's brown bare shoulders. If Zane hadn't pulled her down the trail, Carrie would have stared after Phillip and that boat until they floated out of sight.

Chapter 6

By the time Carrie's birthday arrived, Carrie, Zane, and Mary Beth had started to fall into a routine. Their schedule became almost as predictable as the six o'clock alarm, seven o'clock bus, seven forty-two homeroom bell of the school year.

While Carrie kept searching for new sounds, and Zane kept searching for the red motorboat, Mary Beth was finally starting to feel at home. As far as she was concerned, not seeing the red motorboat again was a good thing, and the lack of sound at the cabin was even better. Especially the lack of one sound. Carrie's dad had no telephone. To call someone she had to walk down the road to the nearest neighbor — a trip that definitely discouraged long inquisitions. Nevertheless, Mary Beth faithfully made the trip on those days she'd promised to call her mother.

"Hi, Mom," sighed Mary Beth as she clutched the receiver. Just as dusk was falling and the bugs were coming out, she'd go to see old Mr.

and Mrs. Pierce and use their phone.

"So tell me all the thrilling things you did today," her mother said. "Was I right? Are you having a terrific time?"

Mary Beth batted away a mosquito. She was sitting on the Pierces' old rocking chair, under the only porch light that had been turned on. Her muscles had a weary, satisfied feel to them and her skin was hot. "We went swimming. I swam across to the other side of the river twice."

"What else?"

"That's about it."

"That's all?"

Mary Beth didn't mention the first two days. Zane throwing herself at "Popeye" and his cartoon buddies. Carrie talking to Phillip, the handsome boy in the rowboat. As usual, she'd been an observer at those events — a bystander who sat back and took in the details. But bystanding wasn't what her mother was interested in. She was interested in the major challenges Mary Beth had taken on in preparation for turning sixteen.

"You must be doing more than just swimming. Have you gone on any big hikes? Seen any wildlife?"

"I don't think so." Mary Beth wasn't sure how to explain that she didn't need to climb Mount Baldy or spot condors. She liked the ordinariness that had settled into these last few days. Snails for breakfast. Mr. Cates dropping them at the beach, where they'd paddle and sunbathe and read. Monopoly. Trivial Pursuit. Zane chattering about the college boys. Carrie writing and singing along with records. Mr. Cates always busy — barbecuing, off running errands, or visiting his many friends.

"Are you doing things you haven't done before?"

"Sort of." In a way, Mary Beth was doing things she'd never done before. The lack of drama allowed her to explore wonderful things. New, quiet things. The cobalt-colored wildflowers that grew under the cabin porch. Clusters of tiny white butterflies. Fat trout that surfaced near the riffles at Mueller's Bend. The way her face felt tight from the sun and was starting to look golden and not quite so babyish.

"Are you really? Honey, this is an important summer for you. Don't waste it by just lying around. Mr. Cates told me about that Fourth of July dance next week. I want you to go. I want you to promise me that you'll do one thing each day that's hard for you. Okay? Just one thing."

Mary Beth went after the mosquito that was still hovering over her forearm and squashed it, smearing blood. What did her mother expect of her? Was she supposed to save children from drowning or skin rattlesnakes?

"Isn't today Carrie's birthday?"

"Yeah."

"Well, are you doing something special?"

"Probably." Mary Beth had been wondering the same thing. So far, Carrie's dad hadn't seemed to remember that today was the important day. "We just got back from the river."

"You remembered to pack Carrie's present, didn't you?"

"Of course."

"Just think, M.B. Soon it will be your turn. Think of all the things that you'll be able to do after you turn — "

"Mom," Mary Beth interrupted. "I have to get off. The Pierces are expecting a call."

"Okay, honey. Call me tomorrow."

"I will. 'Bye." Mary Beth dropped the receiver onto the cradle. The Pierces weren't expecting any calls, and Mary Beth didn't know why she never said what she was really thinking. Why hadn't she told her mother that she would face life in her own sweet time? Why hadn't she said that she looked forward to turning sixteen about as much as she looked forward to parallel parking or taking her SAT's? Why hadn't she explained that she was really having a good time, now that those first two crazy days were over. Why did she always let people steamroll and misread her?

She thanked Mr. and Mrs. Pierce, then walked back down the road, trudging up the steps to the edge of the porch. She sat and dangled her bare freckled legs. People underestimated her because she sat back so much of the time, or blurted out nervous things that made her sound like a baby. But by sitting back and watching, Mary Beth noticed things. By reading books she learned about the world. By stretching her imagination she had developed a talent for filling in the blanks.

Like this evening. Mary Beth knew that she

was the only one who was at all content. Zane was restless. Zane was always restless, but tonight she was doing stomach crunches with violent intensity. Each day at the river, Zane had led the girls on walks. But she never noticed the fragrant grass, or the rocks with gold streaks in them. Mary Beth knew why. Zane was worried that Popeye and his buddies were avoiding her. Except for one blurry pass of their sparkly red motorboat, the girls hadn't seen them again.

And Mary Beth knew that Carrie had a lot on her mind. Of course they were all waiting to see if something would happen for her birthday. But Mary Beth knew there was more to it. Carrie was feeling left behind by her father. Her dad seemed to know everyone at the river. A fellow teacher or neighbor from the city was always up for a visit. Dan just kept hugging Carrie, saying how happy he was to have her there and how wonderful it was for her to be on her own. Carrie still hadn't been able to just sit and talk with him. She still hadn't found the time to discuss her plans to move in with him now that she'd turned sixteen.

Working up the courage to finally say one tenth of what was in her quick, perceptive brain, Mary Beth gestured to Carrie again. "Hey, Carrie!"

Carrie was playing stop-and-go with her Walkman while scribbling on a notepad. She turned off her tape player and looked up. Then she took the tape out, staring at it as if she'd never seen one before. "Hm?"

Mary Beth hesitated. "Do you want to open your presents from us now?"

"Not quite yet." Carrie let her hair cover her face and went back to her writing pad. She'd been thinking about her birthday all day, while waiting for her father. She'd been examining and wondering how she had changed, how she would change. So far she hadn't developed a richer voice, or even a curvier figure or a sharper wit. She'd been on the lookout for some miraculous transformation, but as of yet . . . *nada*. And yet, even with all that whirling around in her mind, there was still room for something else. Or rather, someone else.

"Listen to the river," Carrie had printed down the side of her paper. She'd also squiggled the likeness of a dark, curly headed boy with bronzy shoulders, long legs, and an odd, distant manner. She hadn't drawn a good likeness of Phillip. The dimples were all wrong, and that sudden warmth that could jump into his eyes was missing. Zane was the best artist, and if Carrie had wanted to she could have asked for help. Except that she'd seen the anger in Phillip's face when Zane had stood up for the college boys.

Carrie didn't have much experience with boys. When she thought about Phillip she got a soft dizzy feeling that made her want to hug herself and yell, just for the sound of it. Maybe that was the change she was looking for. This new feeling, a feeling she hadn't experienced before turning sixteen.

"CARRIIEEEE! HELLOO EVERYBODY!"

Carrie's thoughts were blasted by her dad's happy bellow and Melvin's bark down on the road. Zane stopped crunching. Carrie closed her notepad and hid it under a stack of old magazines. Mary Beth stood up, and a moment later, Melvin was leaping, yapping like crazy, and licking Mary Beth's sunburned face.

"It's Mel the monster," Mary Beth giggled. "Are you ever quiet, you crazy dog?"

"Hey, Mel, what's up?" Zane held Melvin's front paws and led him in a dance.

"Dad!" Carrie cried, her heart taking off when she saw him appear on the porch. He was carrying a handful of metallic balloons and a pink bakery box. A ribbon was wrapped around his body as if he were a human present. The numbers "16" were printed on his forehead and when he opened his arms to hug her, the balloons almost floated into space. "You remembered!"

"I remembered," he grinned. "Of course I remembered. How many daughters do I have? How many times do you turn sixteen?"

Carrie ran to throw herself into his arms. But then she stopped, as abruptly as if she'd slammed into a concrete wall. She stared, her mouth falling slightly open. Her father wasn't alone. Standing just to one side of him was a woman in her early twenties. The woman now held the balloons, and looked like she didn't quite know what to do with them. She had short, slightly punk-style hair and a wide, pale face accented with red lipstick. She looked very "city" in black cotton tights and a dark, loose jumper.

Mr. Cates stepped aside to let the young woman onto the porch. "This is Leslie Shurtliff. Leslie was a student of mine last year . . ." He paused and checked with Leslie, not quite able to remember exactly when she'd been in his class.

"Yup. English 401," Leslie reminded him. "I got a B."

Mary Beth and Zane laughed. Carrie had no idea what they found funny.

"Leslie needs a place to crash. All summer there's usually somebody on that porch sofa. Leslie has some friends coming later, too, right?" He checked with Leslie.

She nodded.

"On my birthday?" Carrie blurted out. "Will all her friends stay here, too?" Then she looked down, embarrassed that she'd said it. She had suddenly realized that she might have to share her father with half of Northern California. On her birthday! She knew how popular her father was, and how he believed in keeping his doors open to everyone. But tonight she would have traded his popularity for that of yucky Mr. Buckner, the solitary science teacher at Sherman High.

Her father slipped his arm around her, but Carrie stood stiff as a tree trunk. "Don't worry. I won't run you out of your room." He instructed Leslie to forage for blankets and pillows and whatever else she needed for her stay on the porch. Then he held Carrie by the shoulders and forced her to face him. "I have a big surprise for you. It's your present. I've been working on this since you got here. Do you want to see it?"

Carrie shrugged sullenly. She was once again sinking into that old Valley muddle of stifling haze. She rubbed her eyes, even though there was no reason to feel as if they were burning. "What is it?"

"You don't sound very excited. And after all the trouble I went to. Maybe I should just forget the whole thing," Mr. Cates teased.

"I want to see it!" said Zane.

"Carrie," Mr. Cates soothed, hugging her and brushing the hair out of her eyes. "Grab a jacket and a pair of shoes. Meet me at the truck."

"Great!" cheered Zane. "We can give our presents when we get back. I'm totally into surprises."

Carrie was falling deeper and deeper. Thoughts of Phillip and the river were swirling into the distance. Suddenly the only things in front of her were her father in his heavy Pendleton shirt and Leslie with the balloons and her persistent, smug smile.

"Carrie can you do this one thing?" Her father forced her to lift her chin.

"Why?"

"For me? Please, Car."

Carrie looked at him. He wasn't smiling anymore, and one side of his mustache was drooped. His blue eyes looked almost as confused as hers and Carrie wasn't sure why she was so angry. She remembered how quickly she made emotional U-turns with Stan and wondered if she was just falling back on some old, stale habit. "Okay," she managed, without much enthusiasm.

"Thanks. Hurry up and get ready. All three of you. Last one in the truck has to ride with Melvin. Leslie, you hold down the fort."

Leslie made herself comfortable on the porch sofa. "Okay."

Zane practically flew into the bedroom and appeared a second later with her zebra sandals and an off-the-shoulder T-shirt. Mary Beth was slower and more cautious, although she was still ready with her tennies and labeled sweater before Carrie was.

Soon they were in the back of the truck, shoulder to shoulder to shoulder to evade the cold wind. In spite of Carrie's father's threat, Melvin sat up front with him. The truck rode down the hill so bumpily that the girls slammed into one another. Mary Beth toppled over when they made a sharp turn off Main Street and into the boat ramp parking lot.

"Everybody out," Mr. Cates commanded, clapping his hands. They dropped onto the blacktop.

It was that eerie time of evening when it was still light, and yet the sun was gone. There was a fuzzy gray cast to everything, and if Carrie looked hard enough she could see that the streetlights were already on. The water was soft-edged as it lapped against the dock, and the opposite bank was melting into the dark trees.

But even the dusk couldn't disguise what was waiting at the ramp. A motorboat. Not a fancy one, like Zane's cartoon college boys owned. Not a homemade rowboat, like Phillip's. But something in-between. It had a used, functional inboard/outboard motor and had been painted with yellow and pink stripes. Plastic dinosaurs were taped to the steering wheel and music paper covered the seats. "CARRIE" was scrawled across the bow and "16" was scribbled all over the motor. Carrie gasped, bringing her palms to her mouth.

Her father hugged her. "You already have a nice guitar, and I couldn't afford a car. So, I got you this. The river version of wheels. It'll stay here, and you can drive it every summer."

Carrie bolted across the lot ahead of everyone. Her insides were exploding with joy, blowing away all the gray and the doubt. Phillip . . . Leslie . . . a million student visitors and friends of her father's evaporated for the moment, replaced by one crazy motorboat. It was the kind of grown-up present that Stan would never even consider. And it would be here for her every summer, which meant that she'd be up at the river every summer.

Zane and Melvin ran, too. But Mary Beth walked slowly, suspiciously, as interested in the dusky parking lot as in Carrie's boat.

"It's not fancy, but it will pull a water-skier," said Mr. Cates. "We could take it out tomorrow."

"Or tonight," cried Zane.

"This is why you've been so busy!" cried Carrie.

Mr. Cates stepped back to survey the boat. "This is it. You said that you felt stuck with Stan, that you couldn't go places on your own." He rocked the boat. Cold water splashed on Mary Beth. "This will unstick you."

"Can I learn to drive it myself?"

"If that's what you want." He laughed, hugging Carrie and lifting her off her feet. "I thought you might want to learn to water-ski first."

"Can we take it out now? Just for a short ride," begged Zane.

He checked with all three of them. Zane was jumping up and down. Carrie was clinging to him and smiling adoringly. Mary Beth was nervously chewing on her thumb.

They untied the boat and dropped into it as it slid away from the dock. Mr. Cates turned the key three, four, five times. The motor whined and coughed, refusing to start until he kicked the dash with his faded deck shoe. Finally they began to chug along, surrounded by the smell of churned-up river bottom and fuel. They rode silently for a few minutes, watching the glassy water, the white wake behind them, and the light disappearing on either shore.

"Now this is what it's all about, isn't it?" Mr. Cates said, stretching to take in the dark beauty of the water and the sky. "This is all you need."

Carrie sighed and snuggled up to him. This was more than a change in her life. This was a major door being opened. She felt as if she were a star stepping out in the clear night sky. "Yes."

"Sing me a song, kid."

Carrie sang in a soft, smooth voice, making up lyrics that rhymed perfectly and popped into her head like dreams. Zane leaned over the side of the boat and dragged her hands through the water. Mary Beth shivered. She wasn't sure why, but she had that scratchy feeling in her stomach again.

Chapter 7

The next afternoon, Zane sat back in the cold river and held onto the tow bar. Her feet were encased in stiff plastic mountings attached to wide, fiberglass water skis. Her long hair was dripping down her back and her life jacket pinched her armpits.

"Remember to keep your skis parallel this time," Mr. Cates yelled to her. He was driving Carrie's boat. He wore a Hawaiian shirt, cut-offs, a Giants' baseball cap, sunglasses, and a triangle of white zinc oxide on his nose.

"What?"

"WEIGHT BACK. SKIS TOGETHER. DON'T LOCK YOUR KNEES."

"GOT IT." Zane took a moment to find her bearings. They were about half a mile down from the swimming area. The shore was thick with ferns and reeds, and the river was so wide that there was room for an island and a half-finished beaver dam.

"You're doing great!" Mary Beth encouraged.

She was waving from the back of the motorboat. It was her job to reel in the tow cord when Zane fell and then throw it back out to her again. "I know you'll make it up this time."

"I'd better," Zane yelled back. "This is getting embarrassing."

"Let us know when you're ready," shouted Carrie. She was the watchperson, signaling her father when to take off and when to swing back after Zane had fallen into the water.

Zane nodded. Her teeth were chattering. Her hands were sore. There was water up her nose, in her ears, and probably filling half her stomach. None of that mattered. She didn't care how many times she splatted on her belly or sank into the boat's wake. She was finally doing something new, something that got her adrenaline pumping. None of the girls had water-skied before. Mary Beth wasn't sure she wanted to try it at all, and Carrie was content to stay in the boat with her father. So Zane got the first try. She'd thrown herself into the water, she was so eager for the experience and so afraid that this vacation was turning into a total bust.

"I'M READY."

"Okay," warned Mr. Cates. "Here we go!"

Zane braced herself. She heard the rumble of the motor and smelled gas fumes along the top of the water. There was a sharp jerk as the rope snapped straight. Zane started to whip forward. But she didn't let herself panic this time and some new sense of balance took over. She fought the rope. She pulled her elbows in and with her strong arms kept the tow bar level. Her skis pushed against the heavy water and her breath stopped as she began to rise and skate along the river surface.

"Keep your skis straight!" Carrie screamed.

Even Mary Beth clapped her hands and yelled excitedly, "You're up, Zane. You're up!"

"AHHHHHH!" Zane held on, her knees bent, her arms quivering. She felt as if she were a race car speeding over a sheet of solid ice. She wasn't sure how she'd managed to get up, but now that she was up, she felt as if nothing could knock her back down.

Carrie and Mary Beth cheered as the boat gently picked up speed. Twice the water bumped Zane, but she rose with each wave and touched back down, still flying fearlessly. Carrie's dad drove past the island and Zane stayed tucked, determined, screaming with her hair flying behind her.

"WOOOOOOOO!!!"

Then Zane heard the motor roar even louder. She grimaced and went quiet, preparing for Dan to really speed up. She was ready. Actually, she was beginning to get bored with the easy, straight line she was skating over the river. But then, instead of hearing her own screams or a rush of wind, she heard a cocky male voice. It came from behind, from the middle of the river.

"Hey, if it isn't Olive Oyl!"

Zane didn't dare turn her head, but she saw Mary Beth staring and frowning and she knew. The extra loud roar wasn't coming from Carrie's boat. She wasn't picking up speed. There was another boat and it was coming close. Recklessly close. It was very red and very fast.

The red boat wooshed by and Zane saw a blur of corn-yellow hair. The Pacific Heights boy waved. His friend with the mirrored sunglasses was driving, and the third boy, a stocky pug-faced jock, lay on his back across the rear deck with his hands behind his head.

Zane gripped the tow bar. It was difficult to think about anything other than staying on her feet, and yet she wanted to look glorious for these boys. Sexy, sleek, and as confident as an Olympic diver. She allowed her gaze to fall back to the water and realized that it was not going to be easy. The wake, choppy and fast, from the red boat was heading straight for her knees. Zane stared down at the waves as if they were sharks or schools of piranha.

She steeled herself for the force of the water, but the splash was so high and so forceful that it knocked her over before she could try and ride the waves. She fell, landing so hard that her entire right side smacked against the water and both skis twisted off. She went under and came up gasping.

It was quiet. Just the squawking of a few birds and her coughing and hard breathing. No more motors. Carrie's boat was slowly drifting toward her. There was a splash as Carrie dove in and swam over.

"Are you okay?"

"No problem," Zane panted. Her whole side

stung, but she didn't want to dwell on it. Especially since she saw the red boat out of the corner of her eye. It was floating halfway between the shore and the island. Carrie recovered one ski and Zane grabbed the other. They dog-paddled back to Carrie's boat. Mary Beth held out the tow rope and a hand to pull them in.

"Those guys shouldn't have driven so close." Mary Beth pulled Carrie up, but Zane stayed in the water.

"You're not hurt, are you?" asked Carrie's father.

"No way." Zane unhooked her life jacket, wiggled out of it, and tossed it into the boat.

"I didn't think you were." He winked.

"You were up for a long time, though."

"Good run."

"Yeah." Zane hung onto the side of the boat and fluttered her legs. As soon as her heartbeat was near normal, she flipped into a somersault, as if the side of the boat were the edge of a swimming pool and she were a freestyle racer. Then she started to swim away from Carrie and her father, toward the red boat.

"Who wants to go for a swim?" she yelled back to them.

They merely stared at her.

As much as Zane wanted their company, she couldn't risk losing this opportunity. "Okay, campers. *Adiós*. Be back soon."

"Zane!" objected Mary Beth.

Zane swam. She wasn't sure if she really wanted to swim over by herself to the red boat.

She'd done the somersault just to see what would happen. Because it was fun having everyone watch and worry about her.

"Zane, where are you . . ."

Zane didn't hear the rest of Mary Beth's question because she had dived under like a seal. She stroked and scissor-kicked, getting breathless right away and realizing that the current was against her, and the distance to the red boat was much farther than it looked. The skiing and the fall had taken a lot out of her. Several times she had to rest. She couldn't get enough air. She considered floating back downstream to Carrie and Mary Beth, but she'd come so far that she decided to keep swimming.

Then she was there, a few yards away from the red boat, and she had a moment of panic. The boys seemed too old to her again. She felt very alone and wondered if she looked ridiculous. The pink streak in her hair probably looked like seaweed and she wasn't wearing any makeup. She realized that she was feeling a little woozy.

Luckily, the blond boy spoke first. "She's not Olive, she's a mermaid." He met her at the edge of the boat but didn't attempt to pull her out of the water. His two friends talked to each other, no more interested in her than in an oil slick washing by.

"Hi, Popeye," Zane managed.

He hooked a step ladder over the side of the boat and perched himself on top of it. He had a wide, muscular chest and pink, peeling shoulders. He wore baggy nylon shorts and had a pair of Vuarnets hanging from a cord around his neck. Zane hooked her feet on the bottom rung and floated. Her muscles felt like jelly.

"I'm Daryl," he told her. His eyes were inky blue, with pale, see-through lashes.

"Hi, Daryl. I thought you were going to take me for a ride on your boat." She wondered how old he really was. Nineteen? Twenty???

He glanced back at his buddies. They were still chatting and ignoring Zane. He said in a softer voice, "Where've you been hiding?"

"I've been on the main beach every day."

He rolled his eyes and looked back at his friends again. "The main beach. What a drag. It's full of babies and old people. We're downtown most nights. How come I've never seen you there?"

Zane smiled and tried to look mysterious. She thought of her dull evenings at the cabin playing Monopoly and Trivial Pursuit.

"Everybody hangs out downtown late. Things don't even start until after eleven. Maybe I'll take you for a ride tonight, if you're around." He leaned over the side of the boat and stared at her.

Zane wanted to tell him that she'd already ridden in a boat at night. She wanted to tell him that she wasn't naive or lacking in experience. But she was hooked to his blue eyes. He smiled and her wooziness turned so powerful that she wanted to laugh and yell at the same time. There was so much energy racing inside her that it felt as if her brain had been overloaded. She couldn't think of anything to say.

So, with Daryl still leaning over the side of the boat, staring at her, she pushed off and kicked up as much water as she could. Swept by the current, she swam back across the river with long, easy strokes. By the time she reached Carrie's boat she could feel a rumble underwater and see the sparkly red boat shoot past. She wasn't sure how she was going to manage it, but her days of playing Monopoly were over.

When it was late enough so that boats were lined up at the ramp, and Carrie's boat was stowed safely in its slip, she and her father walked across the dock parking lot. A few clouds sat in front of the sun and there was a sleepy, five o'clock sluggishness as boaters packed up and pulled their crafts out of the water.

"Thanks, Dad," said Carrie. Zane had dragged Mary Beth over to the roller rink, exploring a sudden interest in the Fourth of July dance. This seemed like the first time that Carrie and her father had been alone since the drive down. She felt light with hope, and yet not quite at ease. "The boat is great."

He put his arm around her. They walked slowly, kicking aside gravel and discarded food wrappers. "You did pretty well on those skis."

"Zane did the best. Maybe we can get M.B. to try tomorrow." She didn't mention it, but she was much more interested in learning to drive the boat than in perfecting her skiing.

Her father laughed. "Maybe."

They kept walking, as silent as if they were strangers. When they passed the bridge they were assaulted by a series of loud pops. At first Carrie thought of cap guns. Then she realized that it was almost July and that someone was getting ready early for Independence Day. There was a whistle and the explosion of a firecracker off in the distance.

Carrie's dad turned onto Main Street. They passed The Sweet Shoppe and Carrie lingered . . . she didn't even realize that she was looking for Phillip until she caught herself gazing into the parlor's front window. But the only person inside was an older man. She was wondering where Phillip was and if she would ever run into him again, when she realized that her dad had crossed to the other side of the street. He was in front of the boat shop window.

Carrie ran after him, dodging a bearded man on a motorcycle, and a Winnebago. There were thoughts inside her that had been forming all day. Even when she'd been in the water, waiting to be dragged to the surface, thoughts of her father and of being sixteen had been hopscotching around her head. Now was the time. If she didn't make a point of talking to him, they would be buying motor oil or groceries and the moment would be gone. She'd always hated the way Stan made such a big deal about discussing things, and yet now she found herself using one of his classic tactics.

"Dad, can we sit here for a few minutes?" She pointed to the two benches in front of the bakery. At breakfast time the benches were packed with summer people. Now the bakery was closed and the trash cans overflowed with sticky white paper and empty coffee cups.

"Sure, kid." He sat across from her. The zinc oxide had worn off his nose. He took off his sunglasses and stuck them in his pocket.

"I guess I just wanted to talk," Carrie forced herself to say. "I was glad Leslie didn't come with us today."

Her father shifted and tugged on his mustache. "Why should Leslie have to come with us?"

Carrie wasn't sure why she'd mentioned Leslie, either. "Or any other people that might show up. I just meant, I'm glad to have some time with you alone."

"Me, too."

They sat smiling at each other. Carrie kicked her bare feet. Her bathing suit was soaking through her sun dress and she could feel wetness along her bottom and her back. "I guess it's been weird at home. With Mom and . . ." Just bringing up the subject made her voice catch. It was hard to talk about because she wasn't exactly sure how to identify the problem. She only knew that she felt as if there were a fence surrounding her this past year, surrounding her body, her imagination, and her spirit.

"Is it Stan?" Her dad was very attentive now.

"Partly. He means well, I guess. He just thinks I'm two years old, that I have to be looked after every second. It's hard getting used to him and that house."

"That figures."

"I get upset and Stan tells me I should take harder classes, or something totally dumb like how I should take singing lessons or learn about opera. He always wants to talk, and then he never understands what I tell him. Sometimes it just makes me so mad that I have to live with him, just because Mom decided to marry him. It's not fair."

Her father listened and nodded.

"I guess that's why I wanted to visit you this summer so badly. Even though I only see you at Christmas usually, I feel like you know who I really am. I feel like you understand me."

"I do."

"And I keep thinking that, well, I guess Mom already told you about this, but I was thinking . . . since I'm sixteen now, maybe I should make some changes. I mean, maybe I should live with you next year. In San Francisco. You and me." She had been talking in such a quick jumble that when her father didn't respond right away, she kept on going. "Don't you think so?"

"Your mother didn't tell me that," he finally said.

"That's just what I mean!" Carrie exploded. "They don't take me seriously. They're not honest with me."

Her dad leaned forward and took her hand. "You would really want to live with me?" His eyes looked sad and a little unsure.

"Of course. Why wouldn't I?"

"Carrie, I have my own life. I've been alone for twelve years. I'm sort of stuck in my ways."

"I know that." Now Carrie was embarrassed, wishing she'd never mentioned Leslie or his friends. Why had she ever made such a big deal out of them? "I don't want to intrude on your life. I can respect you, just like you do me. Don't you think I can?"

"Sure." He touched the top of her head and they both leaned forward until their foreheads were almost together. "I love you, kid."

Carrie felt a tug in her throat. A tear slipped down. "I love you too, Dad."

He looked as if he might cry, too. Abruptly, he stood up and held out a hand for Carrie. "Come on. Enough talking. Let's get something to eat."

"Really?"

"I'm starving."

"Okay."

He led the way back across the street. Carrie wasn't quite sure how things had ended. He hadn't definitely said yes, but he certainly hadn't said no. Stan always said that when you grew up you saw less black and white and more of the grays. Maybe this kind of in-between was what he meant. Still, she had to feel some triumph. She'd told him. She'd said it. He loved her, and he understood. She wove through two parked cars, dragging her fingertips and leaving wavy lines on a dusty windshield.

Her mind was so full that she almost didn't realize she was standing right in the way of a rusty ten-speed bicycle, which looked like it had been put together from three different bicycles, with racing handlebars and a water bottle on the frame. It had clipped in front of her as she hopped up onto the sidewalk. She heard a repetitive click and saw that there was a playing card stuck in the spokes of one of the wheels. Somehow she knew that the rider had to be Phillip.

It was.

At first he didn't see her. He coasted on the bike into The Sweet Shoppe's parking lot. She watched him take folded white slacks and a shirt out of his canvas sack. He wore hiking shorts and a nylon jacket with lots of pockets. Gracefully, he collected his things and knelt to lock up his bike. When he finally noticed her, he almost knocked his bike over.

"You go ahead, Dad," Carrie breathed.

"Okay," her father said. "I'll get you something."

Her dad hopped the front steps and disappeared into the shop. Phillip slowly walked by Carrie on his way into work. For a few long seconds they were ultra aware of one another. It felt as if they were the two tin can ends of those telephones Carrie'd made as a kid, tied together by conducting string.

"Hi," he said, stopping and smiling.

"Hi." Carrie stared at the ground. Her heart had begun to thump in her chest. "Done any listening lately?"

His dimples dug in. "Always. You can never listen too much."

"I guess not." Carrie laughed. "So. We finally ran into each other again."

"Yeah." He kicked the gravel as if he were suddenly embarrassed. "You're a hard person to find."

"Not if you look."

"Actually, I did look," he admitted shyly. "Over at Mueller's Bend."

Carrie's face went burning hot. "You did?"

"Up on the bluff. Where those big boulders are. I go up there a lot."

"I haven't been back there."

"That's too bad."

They were both grinning now, and Carrie got tne feeling that neither of them knew just what to say next. Phillip checked his watch.

"Are you late?"

He nodded.

A bell jangled against a glass door. Carrie saw a tall, older man tapping The Sweet Shoppe door from the inside.

"My father," Phillip said.

"Mine, too," Carrie answered in some weird kind of shorthand.

They stood for another moment and then Phillip started to jog away. After a few strides, he turned back. "Listen, maybe we could meet up sometime. At the bend. Or downtown. I work until twelve. I work most of the time, but maybe we can figure it out."

"Okay."

His father tapped the door again, and Phillip waved him off. "I have to go. Let's just meet up somewhere. This isn't a very big town. You're not leaving in the next few days are you?"

"No."

"Good. We'll find each other."

Phillip ran into The Sweet Shoppe. The bell jangled as the door opened and closed. Carrie almost had to sit down on the ground, her heart was beating so fiercely and her breath was so light and shallow. This was another new feeling, one that felt like her entire life was taking a giant U-turn. Phillip hadn't exactly asked her for a date, and yet she knew that somehow, some way, she was going to see him again. She covered her face when she realized that her cheeks were probably red and that she was standing alone in the parking lot, laughing out loud.

Life *had* changed, she realized. She had changed. She wasn't sure when it had happened, but the world had become a pretty wonderful place since she'd finally turned sixteen.

Chapter 8

Zane was supposed to be asleep. She had stretched out across the sleeping bag with her toes touching the bottom seam and her pillow rolled under her head like a basketball. Between the occasional buzz of a mosquito and the rustling of the leaves, she could hear Mary Beth's repetitious breathing and the movements of dreamy, sleepy bodies. M.B. and Carrie were obviously tired from their first day of boating and skiing, but Zane didn't envy them their rest . . . not for a second. In fact she wouldn't trade places, even if it meant turning into the world's biggest insomniac. If anything, Zane wanted to be more wide awake. Electrified. She wanted every thought, every sensation to stay as vivid as lightning.

Zane kicked her sleeping bag and took a deep breath. It hadn't been easy keeping her mind focused because Carrie and Mary Beth didn't understand. Zane was good at clinging to things that were important. She'd hung on to the memory of this day through a dinner of leftover birthday cake and tuna fish sandwiches, then made sure to keep it through the dishes, Monopoly, Leslie's dumb jokes, and getting ready for bed. When Carrie and Mary Beth went to sleep, Zane played all of it back in her head. She felt the gentle rocking of the waves against the boat, the sound of the boys' cocky yells, the trembly strength of her muscles as she skidded over the water. Finally, and most important, she replayed the high-watt excitement she'd felt that afternoon when she'd caught Daryl looking at her with those liquidy blue eyes.

But now the reason for keeping those sensations and memories in front of her had become clear. She'd have to be quick and she'd have to be brave. If she didn't think about Daryl, she'd go chicken and lose her nerve, then slowly drift into sleep, with the possibility that tomorrow things might never happen. She needed to take control. She pushed the pillow away and sat up in her sleeping bag.

"Psssssst, you guys . . ." she whispered from her mattress on the floor.

Carrie and Mary Beth were still asleep. But Zane was ready for that. She'd wake them up even if it took a full marching band.

"Are you awake, campers? Carrie, I bet you are."

Carrie didn't answer.

Zane pushed down her sleeping bag and tiptoed over to the bed. Mary Beth was facing the wall, her arms tangled around her pillow. Carrie lay neatly on her back, hair smooth, face composed.

"I'll bet you three snails, sixteen games of Clue, and one red motorboat that you're going to wake up. Or that you're awake already." Zane walked her fingers up Carrie's arm.

Sure enough, Carrie's eyes flapped open.

"Faker."

"Hi, Zane."

"Hi."

"What's up?"

"I'm going nuts, Carrie."

"What else is new?"

"I can't sleep."

"Me, neither."

"Good. I like company. What are you thinking about?"

Carrie grinned, then covered her face with her pillow. When she refused to uncover it, Zane felt her excitement fade. Zane hated it when Carrie refused to confide in her. Carrie'd been acting secretive since they'd arrived home after water skiing. It made Zane feel lonely and unimportant. Especially now, when it seemed like the whole world was bubbling up inside of her. "Is something wrong?" Zane asked.

"No." Carrie lifted the pillow. "Everything is right."

"Like what?"

"Just everything."

Zane sat for a while listening to the jumpy crickets. Her antsiness had dulled and she longed to crank it up again. When she was flying with high voltage she didn't worry about feeling left out or ignored. "It's not even midnight." Zane watched Mary Beth for a minute. "M.B.," she teased, tickling the short hairs on the back of Mary Beth's neck. Mary Beth mumbled and brushed Zane's hand away.

"Don't wake her up." Carrie sat, holding the sleeping bag around her shoulders. A cool breeze fluttered the curtains. Somewhere in the distance a firecracker popped.

"Why?" Zane felt so impatient now that her knees jiggled and her fingers drummed against her thighs. She lurched across Carrie and shook Mary Beth.

"HHHAA . . ." Mary Beth awoke with a terrified start. "Wha . . . Where . . ." Her short hair was pressed flat to one side of her head and she stared at Zane and Carrie, as if she had no idea who they were.

"It's just us, M.B. Don't freak out."

"Zane, you shouldn't have woken her."

"We have our whole lives to sleep."

"Why did you wake me?" Mary Beth rubbed her face. "I think I was having a bad dream."

"That's why I woke you. So you could stop having your bad dream."

"Zane."

"SHHHHHH!!!"

Zane's warning was so urgent that they all froze in a huddle. She had heard footsteps in the living room and waited for Carrie's father to approach the kitchen and the hall. She braced herself for an order to stop horsing around, settle down, and go to sleep. But instead, someone played soft music on the stereo and the footsteps made their way back to the other end of the cabin. When the girls leaned in to speak again, jazz piano camouflaged their voices.

"Do you guys realize that we've been here for over a week already?" Zane whispered.

"So?"

"So. Carrie's already sixteen. You may want to turn sixteen without having anything ever happen to you, M.B. But, I don't! We'll have to go home soon."

"Not for good," said Carrie. "Not me."

Zane looked at her. Maybe that was it. Maybe Carrie was gloating over the move, preparing herself to move away from the Valley and her best friends. Maybe she was moving away a little at a time, so she wouldn't have to do it all at once.

"Did you tell your dad that you wanted to move in with him?" Mary Beth asked.

Carrie nodded.

"What did he say?"

"He said of course. He'd love for me to live with him. It's up to me."

They were quiet again, pondering the reality of such a bold, brave decision. Then Zane took action, the water and the boat coming back into focus. She prodded the mattress with her finger. "So we don't have much time left." She stood up and started rustling through her clothes, which were in a sloppy mound on the floor. She held various articles up to identify them in the single ray of porch light. With Carrie and Mary Beth staring, she whipped off her night shirt and replaced it with a tank top and tie-dyed jeans.

"What are you doing?"

"I'm sneaking out. I'm going downtown."

"What? Zane!"

"Shh!"

Mary Beth spoke more softly. "Now? You're going downtown now?"

"Yes. Are you coming with me or not?"

Mary Beth looked terrified. She'd seen Zane get that wild-eyed look before, and she knew how hard it could be to change Zane's mind — like the time Zane had convinced M.B. to visit the fortune-teller on Santa Monica pier, or the day when the three of them had cut a half day of school to ride George Ellis's motorcycle. "Why do you want to go downtown now? It's so late."

"Mary Beth!" Zane angrily brushed her hair. "Haven't you noticed that we are the only people who aren't downtown at night?"

"How do you know? We've never *been* downtown at night."

"That's just what I mean. We're the only ones on the beach in the day who are over the age of twelve and under the age of thirty."

"No, we're not."

"M.B., we are. I think we should celebrate Carrie's birthday. Come on."

"How are we going to get down there?"

"We can walk. It's not even a mile."

"Why don't we ask Mr. Cates if he'd take us." Mary Beth looked to Carrie, pleading for her to step in and put a stop to Zane's craziness. "He always says we can do what we want."

But Carrie had a far-off look of her own. Wistful. Dreamy. Expectant.

"Let's talk to your dad," Mary Beth urged.

"No," Carrie responded in a decisive voice. "Don't bother my dad. He doesn't need to chauffeur us around all the time. He has his own life." There was no way she'd bother her father. She'd prove to him she wouldn't be intruding on his life.

Zane grinned and hopped back on the bed. "So we're going? We'll sneak out and walk downtown?"

Carrie got up and checked the bedroom window. It was low to the ground and easy to open. No screen. Her skin was tingling with fear and yet she was leaning toward the open air. "Maybe we should," she grinned. "To celebrate my birthday." Then the fear hit her again. Hard. She turned back and pointed sternly at Zane. "We're not staying down there for long, though. Just long enough to look around. To see what's going on. That's all."

"And if we get in trouble . . ."

"M.B., would you stop being such a wimp!"

"I'm not a wimp!" Mary Beth looked hurt. She hugged her stomach for a moment, then started to peel off her sleeping bag. "All right. Let's go."

They dressed in the dark, using flashlights to fix their hair and little pocket mirrors to dab on touches of makeup. Trying desperately to keep quiet, they stuffed clothes and pillows in their empty sleeping bags. Carrie smacked her shin on the bed frame and Zane got the giggles.

"SHHH!"

They opened the window, holding their breath as the old wooden frame creaked and rattled, and climbed out onto the porch.

"What about Melvin?"

They all froze as Melvin began to bay and howl. But nothing else happened. Melvin always bayed and howled, so maybe Carrie's father didn't pay much attention to him. Finally Melvin quieted and they kept going, commando style, praying to arrive safely at the stairs. When they were almost across the porch, Zane glanced back. Melvin stood on the porch, sniffing around. The music was still going and Carrie's father was talking to Leslie.

They negotiated the wooden steps awkwardly in the pitch dark. The brambles scratched their arms and Mary Beth stumbled more than once. Then suddenly they were on the road, the dirt path to adventure unrolling before them. Giddy, they began to run.

"Let's go, campers!!!!"

Zane led the way, racing like a crazy person, until she stopped to catch her breath. That was when she saw Carrie speed up ahead of her.

"ROCK AND ROLLLLLLL . . ."

The jacked-up Chevrolet, fat-tired and fuzzy-diced, squealed around the corner and past the girls like a banshee howling from beneath the earth. It didn't make it any less scary that a boy was leaning out the back window, yelling his head off. Mary Beth flinched and huddled closer to Zane. Carrie stared at the car, but Zane kept walking as if nothing unusual was happening. All three of them were high on adrenaline and late-night giddiness.

"Are you guys sure that this is okay?" Mary Beth said in a shaky voice.

"Sure, M.B. They're just locals."

"Locals?"

"They're just lowlifes who live here all year round. Besides, what are you afraid of? Nothing's ever going to happen." Zane moaned. "That's the whole problem. Nothing ever happens."

"Stuff happens," Mary Beth insisted.

"Like what?"

"Lots of things, Zane. I don't know what it is you want."

Zane almost threw herself onto the sidewalk. Walking backward she gestured to Mary Beth. "SOMETHING! Something exciting. Mary Beth, have you ever had anything exciting happen to you? Ever?"

"Well . . ." Mary Beth stopped to think. "Right before I left I had to clean out my aquarium. I held the fish in the little net to get them out and I dropped one. So I gave it artificial respiration." She twisted her mouth up in a coy grin. "If that isn't a thrill, I don't know what is."

When Zane and Carrie realized that Mary Beth was making fun of herself, they all laughed together. The noisy car and the tension they felt from sneaking out of the house eased. Once again they were the trio that had been famous at Sherman High for their togetherness and private jokes.

"That is pretty exciting, M.B."

"I know. You always underestimate me, Zane."

Zane hugged her and Mary Beth gave Zane a mock slug.

"So, where should we go first?"

They looked around and noticed that the town didn't look all that different at night. Probably the noisiest place was the Watering Hole Tavern, which overflowed with music, old men, and "over twenty-one" college students. No one was eager to start there. On the other hand, the only teenagers seemed to be sitting on the curb in front of the roller rink.

"Listen," Carrie said, taking charge as they crossed the street and approached the rink. "We're just seeing what's going on, remember? Checking things out. I don't want to stay here for long. Let's split up and meet back in fifteen minutes. Then we race home and pray my father doesn't kill us."

"You mean we have to go off on our own?"

Carrie's eyes looked determined but evasive. "M.B., you go with Zane."

"You can tell me more of your exciting life, M.B.," Zane teased.

"I can't believe I have to be seen with you," Mary Beth came back.

Zane posed against the lamppost. "I know I'm

a hard act to follow." She started to push Mary Beth toward the bridge.

Mary Beth refused to budge. "No getting on any boats, Zane! We have to be back here in fifteen minutes. Okay?"

Zane batted her eyes. "Okay." Suddenly she grabbed Mary Beth's arm and ran, pulling her down the sidewalk, in the direction of the boat dock.

"Carrieeeee, save meeee . . ." M.B. yelled in a nervous, giggly voice. But there was no stopping Zane, and both girls soon disappeared.

Carrie watched them go, then with a breathless, unsettled feeling inside, she walked away from the roller rink and straight toward The Sweet Shoppe. She hadn't meant to be so devious, and yet with Zane and Mary Beth she sometimes had to evade the real issue. Especially after Zane made that awful comment about "low-life locals." Sure, Zane and M.B. were her best friends. But there were some things she had to do on her own.

"I hope I'm not doing something truly dumb," she prayed as she walked down the shadowy sidewalk away from the noisy tavern, past the boat shop and the bakery and the empty market parking lot.

Carrie had made up her mind as soon as Zane mentioned the idea of sneaking out. Even though she knew she was deceiving her dad, she wanted to see Phillip. She *had* to see Phillip. Sure, they should have asked her dad to take them. But she hadn't wanted her father to feel that if she lived with him, she would be a nuisance or a nag. She had to learn to do things on her own.

Carrie ran across the street, ignoring the kids in front of the skating rink. The wind was blowing harder and the trees shook as if they were cold. She walked past a metal trash bin, a couple of empty newspaper stands, and then hopped the steps onto the sidewalk that led to The Sweet Shoppe. Her floppy boots made hardly any sound against the concrete, and her shadow looked ten feet long. Carrie wondered for an instant whether she should turn around, but before she had time to decide, she was in front of the ice cream store. The light coming through the windows was cold and white, the reflection from the long silver freezers. Carrie sighed. It was only a night-light, a lamp to keep away burglars. She was too late. Phillip was gone.

Carrie sunk down on the front step and held her face in her hands. She wanted to laugh and cry at the same time. She was still scared from sneaking out, disappointed that Phillip wasn't there and relieved at the same time. After all, what was she going to say to him? And what if he hadn't meant it about wanting to meet up with her again? She was about to get up when she heard an odd clackity-clack sound. It made her think of castanets or those clicking metal noise-makers they'd given as birthday favors when she was a kid.

"Is that you?" she heard.

Carrie turned and saw a boy walking his bicycle around from the other side of the store. When he stepped under the street lamp she saw his dark curly hair, a chocolate-stained white shirt tied around his waist, and a ten-speed bike with a baseball card stuck in the spokes of the rear wheel.

Chapter 9

A car horn blasted somewhere on Main Street. Stuck, it continued to blare. Carrie and Phillip stared at the street until the noise finally bleep-bleeped, then trickled out. Carrie giggled from embarrassment. Her cheeks were burning hot, and it wasn't from the sun. Now that she had found Phillip, she felt as if she were wearing a signboard around her neck. One that read, "I like you! I'm attracted to you. I've snuck all the way down here just to see you." Even with her limited sixteen years of experience, she knew that this was the essence of uncool.

"We meet again," Phillip said, finally. He seemed surprised. He would glance at her, then down at his bike, as if he weren't sure what to make of running into her again.

"What a coincidence." As soon as the words were out of Carrie's mouth, she felt like a fool. Why else would she be here except to intercept Phillip when he got off work?

"I'm glad you found me. I just closed up."

"You are? You did?"

"Well, about ten minutes ago. What are you doing down here?"

"Oh, just exploring. You know me, I stand by myself in pretty odd places."

He smiled. His stiff posture relaxed and he leaned forward over the handlebars. "I guess you do. I hope you weren't listening again. Not here."

They were quiet for a moment. Tires squealed. A trash can blew over. A firecracker whistled and sent a chill down Carrie's spine. "Not here."

Phillip climbed off his bike. Then he glanced around, as if he expected someone to be hiding in the shadows or behind the Dumpster. "Where are your friends?"

"My friends?" Carrie wasn't quite sure how to answer. She didn't know who Phillip thought her friends were. She wanted to explain that she had nothing to do with the college boys. But that would also have meant explaining Zane. How could she explain that the girl who had stood up against Phillip had been one of her best friends since seventh grade? "I'm meeting them later," she told him. "I thought I'd explore on my own."

Phillip rested his bike against the wall of the shop. He slowly sat down on the steps leading to The Sweet Shoppe's side door and began scratching little squiggles in the dust with a Popsicle stick. "Good." He was drawing a fish. It looked like a cave drawing or a cartoon. "You don't seem to be like them." He glanced at her, his green eyes settling on her face. He took all of her in, her eyes, her cheeks, her mouth, her chin. "Are you?"

Carrie hesitated. His eyes did something to her. It had been the same way when she'd seen him in his rowboat. Her legs went slightly unstable and the air around her seemed to change texture. She sat down next to him, too nervous to get very close. "Sometimes people aren't what they seem."

Phillip scratched a dot of frosting off his hand. "Sometimes they're exactly what they seem."

Carrie found a Popsicle stick and began squiggling, too. Anything to keep her mind off the breezy dark and the nearness of Phillip's shoulder. The squiggles became double squiggles. "Sometimes people just don't think," she tried to explain.

"Or care. Or see. Or listen. There," Phillip said, turning her squiggle into a face.

Carrie added glasses. Phillip added a beard and Carrie squiggled a top hat. "This is like arts-and-crafts camp."

"Really?" Phillip looked puzzled.

"I guess you never went to summer camp. I mean, why would you need to, living here?"

He gazed down toward the river. His face took on a pensive, determined quality. He reminded Carrie of herself when she was trying to talk to her father or write a song.

"Did you grow up here?" she asked him.

"Yes." Phillip placed his Popsicle stick and

some discarded foil around the neck of their squiggle like a collar and tie.

"Did you like it? I think it'd be great."

"It had its moments." Phillip leaned back on the step and smiled. "Like Mr. Kawaki. He was my teacher from fifth to eighth grade. Up here grade school goes from K through 8."

"It does?"

"It does. Anyway, Mr. Kawaki had bluish hair and everyone said he used hair dye. His wife was supposed to be a flamenco dancer, and there was a picture of her on his desk and she had a rose between her teeth."

"No," Carrie laughed. "I thought all the weirdos were supposed to live in L.A.!"

"I thought so, too." He smoothed away some of their squiggles with his track shoe. "Actually, Mr. Kawaki was pretty smart. Even though we were just kids, he used to take us on these walks every day. He'd tell us about the plants, the rock formations, the Indians that used to live near here. There was this amazing meadow up on top of Headly Butte." Phillip pointed to the hills across the river. "It was the most beautiful place I think I've ever seen. Two kinds of wildflowers grew there that don't grow anywhere else along the river. Now there are summer cabins there." He looked at her and Carrie could see the passion in his eyes. Then he shrugged and began to laugh. "I can't believe I'm sitting here talking about Mr. Kawaki! You and I have the weirdest conversations."

Carrie grinned. She was fascinated with Mr. Kawaki. At this moment, Mr. Kawaki was the most interesting subject on earth. "We do, don't we?"

"You don't care about this," he insisted, turning away and kicking the foil and Popsicle sticks into the parking lot. "No one does. I shouldn't care so much about it, either."

"Why do you say that?"

"Because my father's right. We can't do anything about it. We should just be happy that all these people come here and not try to change things."

His angry voice and clenched fists roused something in Carrie. It reminded her of her own frustration with Stan, which came flooding back like an electrical charge. "Why can't we change things?" she heard herself argue. "We're sixteen! At least I am. My father is changing things for me, I know he is. What's the point of turning sixteen if everything has to go on the same old way?"

He was facing her now, gesturing angrily and staring right into her eyes. "Sixteen doesn't help. It gets back to weird Mr. Kawaki and my father. Mr. Kawaki is now a counselor at my high school. He's the only counselor, actually — and he also teaches math and metal shop. He found out about this workshop in San Jose this August. It's this three-week intensive thing, a sort of introduction to studying the environment. I'm eligible for it because I'm sixteen — I'm almost seventeen, actually — but my father wouldn't let me go."

"He wouldn't?"

"Well, he didn't forbid it exactly. He just said that it was pointless, that there was no changing things. It's progress, he says. And he needed me in the shop. So here I am. And here I'll stay."

"But you're sixteen," Carrie repeated. "You should be able to decide for yourself! Your father sounds like Stan."

He paused. "Who's Stan?"

"My stepfather. He makes sure that nothing changes before you turn sixteen."

"And then what?"

Carrie felt her mouth turn up in a funny, self-conscious smile. "Gee. I don't know. I've only been sixteen for one day."

"Really?" Phillip nudged her with his shoulder. "One day, huh?"

"One day."

"So I guess that's why you're such an expert."

"I guess so."

"Well. Happy birthday."

Carrie shrugged and an odd thing began to happen. She started to laugh. It was a giddy, free laugh, the kind of laugh she usually only shared with Zane and Mary Beth. There was so much fizzy energy buzzing around inside her that she had to either laugh or scream her head off. As if he knew what was going on inside her, Phillip began to laugh, too. The corners of his mouth perked up enough to push those deep dimples into his cheeks. Their giggling overlapped with the rumble of the cars, the firecrackers, and the rowdy men leaving the Watering Hole Tavern. The sound of their combined laughter was the most musical thing that Carrie had heard since she'd been to Watson River.

Phillip leaned closer and touched her hand. It was somewhere between a stroke and a tap. The laughter stopped, replaced by quiet breathing and that current flowing between them. "Hey, want to walk me home?" he asked suddenly. "I know it's not very exciting, but it's only two blocks. That is, unless you have to meet your friends now."

"Not yet."

"Really? You'll walk home with me?"

"Sure."

"Great. Let's go."

They got up and started walking. Phillip moved the bicycle to his side. The card in the spokes ticked away like a clock, but Carrie didn't feel as if she were being timed, or measured in any way. Instead it was a steady, warm accompaniment, like a snare drum or an acoustical bass. They headed off Main Street and down a narrow dirt path. Soon it was just the bike, the moon, and the sweet-smelling blackberry bushes.

They stopped in front of a wood-shingled house. It was small, in need of new paint. There was a room above the garage, and an old station wagon parked in the driveway. When Carrie looked past the garage, she saw that the rear of the house bordered the river. Phillip's rowboat was tied to the small dock in back.

They stood for a moment, the moonlight flooding their faces. Neither of them could say good night yet, but they weren't sure what to say instead. Phillip rested his bike against the peeling picket fence, then joined her in the dirt road, next to the neighbor's rosebushes. The air was breezy and full of perfume.

"So. Tell me more about you. Tell me about Stan and L.A. Tell me about your father and turning sixteen."

Carrie smiled for what seemed like the hundredth time that night. She thought for a moment as a raccoon rustled out of the rosebushes and shot across the dirt lane. "The most important thing about me is that I want to do something special, I guess. To write a song where the music and the lyrics fit together perfectly. Where it starts to tell a story, and then suddenly, without knowing it, you're sucked in and living in this tiny world of a song."

"Like the tiny world of this town."

"Yes! But I can't do it if Stan never lets me do anything. That's why being up here is so important. That's why I have to move in with my dad now. I have to be able to change, to break free. Do you know what I mean?"

Phillip nodded slowly. He was gazing at her again, with such directness that Carrie almost took a step back. And yet her feet were planted. Her legs were woozy, but her feet had no desire to move.

"I think I do know what you mean," he said.

Phillip took a step closer to her. His nylon parka fluttered in the breeze. Carrie stood very still as the wind blew her hair across her mouth.

She shivered slightly and Phillip put his hands on her shoulders. The warmth of his palms flowed down her arms, through her whole body. They stood like that as the moment stretched out of shape, into something soft and formless, timeless and steady as the river water.

It all speeded up again when the curtains parted in Phillip's living room window. Light sprayed out onto the street, illuminating the two of them, Phillip's bike, and the dial on his wristwatch.

"Oh, no!" Carrie gasped.

"What's wrong?"

"How did it get so late!" Carrie froze. For a moment she wasn't sure which direction led back to Main Street. "I have to go. Right now."

"Where?"

As much as Carrie didn't want to leave him, she still didn't want to put him together with Zane. "I just have to go back to the roller rink. Really."

"I'll go with you."

"No."

"Are you sure?"

Carrie nodded. She was facing uphill, but wasn't quite able to get her body to move. "Maybe I'll see you at the beach."

"I'm about to get incredibly busy at the store. With the Fourth coming up, things get crazy here. Maybe I'll find you above Mueller's Bend. Where's your father's cabin?"

Carrie couldn't answer. The mention of her father's cabin had made the reality of this night slide down on her like an avalanche. She began to run up the lane now, making a spray of dust and rocks. She heard Phillip yell something . . . good-bye, or maybe good night. She didn't stop. Her arms and legs were on fire with this whole night. She remembered again how late it was. How dangerously late. Before now, she hadn't thought about getting back to the cabin, or back into her bedroom. Please don't let us get caught, she chanted. Please don't let my father find out. Then she flew down Main Street. Throwing back her head, she ran with all she had. Still, she smiled. Even if she did get caught, it would be worth it.

Chapter 10

"So where's Carrie?"

"She'll be here soon."

"When?"

"I don't know!"

"She's late."

"Zane!"

"Great! I rush to get back here — maybe blow my entire chance with Daryl — and she's not even here!"

"Zane, just cool out."

The scratchy feeling inside Mary Beth was turning fierce. Now it was corn husks, or itchy wool army blankets. But what could she do about it? Nothing, so she and Zane sat on the curb in front of the roller rink, which was littered with flyers announcing the upcoming dance, a box of Uncle Sam's Sparklers, and squashed cigarette butts. Foamy water trickled down the gutter. It was almost one o'clock and Main Street was becoming deserted. The other kids had either left or gone inside to skate to muffled versions of

Elton John tunes and the Bunny Hop.

Mary Beth picked up the sparkler box. It was empty. Good. The last thing she needed was more fireworks. The later it became, the wilder Zane was acting. She was getting so charged up she might have been the exploding American flag at the end of a Fourth of July display.

"Sometimes Carrie drives me crazy," Zane ranted. "She acts so moody, then she won't tell me what's bothering her. She gets all uptight about coming downtown and says we can't stay long. And now where is she?" Zane twisted her earring, clapped her sandals together, huffed, and kicked the curb. She made Mary Beth think of a battery-operated toy on overdrive.

Mary Beth, however, felt like someone who had run out of gas. That bristle in her stomach was making her wonder why she'd let Zane talk her into this late-night excursion. What was it about her personality that made her such a sucker? She knew she didn't want to sneak out and come down here, and yet, when push came to shove, there she was, jumping out the window and tripping down the road with the rest of them.

The worst part was that Mary Beth never felt a part of these escapades when they happened. She always felt slightly seasick, and on the outside — as if she were watching a movie that she knew was going to get gory and disgusting. Like the time Zane made them run through Balboa Park, spray painting the chain link fences. Mary Beth went along, only to throw up behind the bushes when she thought she saw a policeman under the basketball hoop. Zane liked company on her wild excursions, and Mary Beth never objected. Not yet anyway. So far she had never stood up and said, "I don't want to be part of this." "I won't even watch." "I'm leaving."

And tonight . . . of course, Zane had had to go to the boat dock first thing. She'd dragged Mary Beth under the bridge, where it was so dark they had to feel their way, touching stone walls that were coated with something slick and gross-smelling. They'd found Daryl and his friends right away. The boys hadn't taken the boat out yet that evening, but instead had been racing around the woods on their all-terrain vehicles. When Zane and Mary Beth discovered them, they were hanging around their truck, covered with dust and sweat.

"Hey, look who's here," Zane had cried with a coyness that made Mary Beth shrivel inside. As if there were any other reason to be at the boat dock besides chasing Daryl and his red motorboat.

"Who's that?" Daryl had answered, in an equally smarmy tone. "Hey." He wolf-whistled. "It's Olive, the mermaid." He'd elbowed his two buddies, whose names turned out to be Matt and Justin.

Matt was the one who looked like the music video addict. Even without his glasses, his eyes were cold and metallic. Justin was the hefty jock, sullen and gruff, much more interested in boats and bikes than two fifteen-year-old girls. Actually, the longer Mary Beth had stood in the shadows watching, the more she got the feeling that Daryl was the only one who wanted to risk being seen with Zane.

"So, are you going out on your boat tonight?" Zane had asked.

Before Daryl could answer, Matt responded flatly, "No. We're just down here to tuck it in. Kiss it good night."

Justin laughed. His laugh sounded like a dog barking, and then Daryl laughed, too. A moment later Zane had forced a giggle as well. After that, Zane had stood around looking self-conscious while the boys locked up their all-terrain vehicles and got the boat ready for their night ride. Zane posed against the truck wheel, shifted her sweater, flung back her hair, and hummed to herself. Once Daryl swooped over to tickle her, grabbing her waist and nuzzling her bare neck. He even asked her name. But his spurt of attention ended when Matt snapped his fingers, ordering him to quit fooling around and fill the gas tank. Throughout this whole charade, Mary Beth watched from behind a street lamp, growing so impatient and annoyed that she thought she would burst.

Finally, Mary Beth had come forward. In a voice that came out like cracked wheat, she reminded Zane of their promise to meet Carrie back at the roller rink. Mary Beth actually sensed that Zane was relieved for an excuse to leave. Now she wouldn't have to admit that the boys were not eager to include her in their midnight outing. But as soon as they crossed under that awful bridge and got back to Main Street, Zane was carrying on as if the romance of the century were being tampered with.

"What if I never see Daryl again?" Zane moaned, leaning forward on the curb to look for Carrie. She rubbed her eyes, grinding mascara down to her cheekbones. "Once we leave, that's it. I'll never get another chance."

Mary Beth wasn't sure why, but it was becoming more difficult for her to stay quietly in the background. Maybe it was being away from her mother. Maybe it was so much of pure unadulterated Zane. Maybe it was fifteen and three-quarter years of swallowing back half of what she really thought and felt. "What would you have done with those three guys on that boat anyway?" she asked in a tiny voice. "In the middle of the night."

Zane's dark eyes looked startled at the purpose behind Mary Beth's words. Then she melted. "You wouldn't understand, Mary Beth."

"Right." Mary Beth felt forced back into silence. She knew what Zane meant. Mary Beth was the innocent. The dummy. The prude. The one boys never paid attention to. Maybe that was true, but Mary Beth also sensed that Zane wasn't nearly as experienced as she pretended to be.

"I wouldn't be with all three of them," Zane came back in a disgusted voice. "I just want to be on that boat with Daryl."

"To do what, Zane? You don't even know him."

Zane hesitated as if she were trying to figure it out herself. But then she fell back onto the sidewalk, laughing and not even noticing that a Tootsie Roll wrapper had become tangled in her hair. "Wouldn't you like to know?" she teased.

I know more than you think! Mary Beth was about to say. But she stopped herself when she heard the tap-slap of hurried feet on pavement and saw a glint of Carrie's blonde hair under the flashing Watering Hole Tavern sign. Carrie dodged two old men who had staggered out of the bar, and waved to Zane and Mary Beth. By the time she reached them she was breathing heavily.

"Sorry I'm late."

"Where have you been?" Zane asked after a moment. "Did something happen?"

Mary Beth was surprised that Zane hadn't gone on the attack, demanding to know why she'd been forced to cut short her rendezvous with Daryl. And yet, as Mary Beth observed Carrie, she knew why. There was a brightness in Carrie's eyes, an openness to her features that made her look incredibly beautiful. For the moment, Carrie wasn't someone you wanted to wrangle with. She looked so elated — not at all like the stopped-up, frustrated Carrie they knew back in L.A.

"We're going to get in so much trouble."

"Mary Beth, cool out. Carrie, we saw Daryl and his friends. It was totally great."

"Tell me about it when we get back," Carrie panted. "Let's go!" She led them in a race down Main Street, even though she wasn't sure she had any energy left. She was aware of the hotness in her lungs and the weariness of her legs, which weren't used to waterskiing and racing in the same day. She remembered that the route home was uphill.

"Carrie, wait up!" begged Mary Beth, as Carrie turned onto the dirt road that led up to the cabin.

Carrie wanted to turn back and yell, "I can't wait up. I can't stop because I'm so full of this person I just talked to. My legs won't slow down and I feel like I could run forever." But then she saw Zane running next to her, passing her, and Carrie knew that she couldn't explain Phillip to Zane. She couldn't risk putting Zane and Phillip together in any combination because they just might ignite like a forest fire.

"Mary Beth, come on," Carrie called in a softer voice, since they were getting closer to the cabin. She stopped and waited, just in case she might have to carry M.B. on her shoulders. Right now she felt capable of doing that. She felt that strong and full of hope.

But Mary Beth didn't need her help after all. M.B. was slow but steady, and when they finally reached Carrie's dad's pickup, which was parked alongside the road, M.B. seemed to be the only one with strength to spare. Zane was panting like crazy now and clutching her side. Carrie's tiredness had just fallen on her like a load of sand.

"Not a sound," Carrie begged.

They started up the stairs very slowly because they had forgotten to bring a flashlight. This time it was Zane who stubbed her toe and Carrie whose skirt caught on a bramble. Time moved as slowly as sludge until they climbed high enough to see the cabin and the porch.

"Shhhh!!!"

When they hit the top stair, Carrie felt her heart crash to the ground. Melvin had started barking and the living room light was on.

"Oh, no," Zane said in too loud a voice.

"Quiet!"

"It's not my fault if we get in trouble," Zane whispered. "You were the one who had to stay down there so long."

Carrie's heart was pounding so hard that she thought it would wake the entire town. What was she *doing*? She could be blowing her entire life, her entire future with her father, right now. She would never have snuck out if Zane hadn't thought of it first. Sure, she had been thinking about Phillip, thinking a lot about Phillip, but she could have seen him another time!

The thing that really sickened her was her dishonesty. It was possible that her dad wouldn't mind that they had gone downtown. But the problem was they had deceived him. Carrie bit back tears as she suddenly realized that it could all be coming to a premature end . . . Phillip . . . the move . . . her boat . . . this magical, musical summer. Kaput, presto, it was all about to dissolve and turn back into a puff of smog.

"I can't move," she said.

They stood, paralyzed on the top stair, while Melvin yapped and bayed. It was as if the porch were mined and no one wanted to take that first damaging step. But then something amazing happened. The porch light flicked off. Just like that. Light, and then total darkness. There was some movement near the cabin door, a rustle out on the porch, and then Carrie's father yelled, "Melvin, be quiet! It's nothing. Go to sleep."

Melvin kept barking.

"Melvin, shut up!"

Melvin whimpered and gradually calmed.

Carrie was still afraid to move. Holding out her arms to prevent Zane and Mary Beth from skirting by her, she stood listening to the crickets and the thrashing of her heart. Finally she took a single step onto the wooden porch.

Nothing happened.

Amazed that she didn't sink or explode, Carrie took another step, so slow and quiet that she thought she might have become invisible. Zane and Mary Beth followed carefully. Not a creak. Not a breath. Not a false step or a sigh.

The bedroom window was still open. Carrie held back the curtains and helped Mary Beth in. She moved quickly and disappeared into the dark bedroom. Zane was next. Carrie popped through last and they almost tumbled over one another. It took a moment for their eyes to adjust. Mary Beth started to close the window. The wood groaned, and Zane yanked Mary Beth's hand away. Carrie frantically motioned for M.B. not to bother. Barely taking the time to strip off their clothes, they pulled out the things they'd stuffed into their sleeping bags and jumped in. Then they lay motionless, listening to the night.

At least five uneventful minutes passed before Zane lifted her head and whispered, "Good night, campers."

The three of them sputtered with hysterical laughter as they stuck their faces in their pillows and pretended to be asleep.

Chapter 11

Nearly a week passed. It turned scorching hot. So hot that no one at the cabin wanted to eat anything besides cantaloupe and frozen fruit bars. Mary Beth developed a heat rash under her arms. Carrie started using sunblock. Melvin moped and lapped up bowl after bowl of water. The cabin felt hemmed in and crowded, and it was so hard to sleep that Leslie put a fan out on the porch.

The only way to survive the afternoons was to stay near the cold glassy water. Carrie, Mary Beth, and Zane avoided the main beach now. Except for water skiing, they hung out above Mueller's Bend. With their towels laid out on the warm, gray rocks, they sunbathed alone on the bluff, or jumped down into the deep water. Mary Beth chattered and read. Zane coated herself with so much cocoa butter that she smelled like a chocolate factory. Carrie took solitary hikes, twice returning with that lovely expression she'd worn when they'd first snuck out of the cabin six days before.

"I don't know if I even want to go to the dance tomorrow night," Zane was complaining. It was Friday, the third of July. A huge American flag hung above the roller rink roof. When the infrequent breeze blew, stars and stripes fluttered across the clear sky.

Mary Beth nudged her. "Now who's being a wimp?"

"Me? Never." Zane lifted her sunglasses and leaned across the crevice between two rocks. Squinting, she peered around the bend, then lay back on her towel and picked at her nail polish. "I think Daryl left. I think he and his friends went back to Pacific Heights."

"Maybe he's just avoiding you."

"Maybe it's *you* they're avoiding, Mary Beth."

Mary Beth giggled. "Maybe. I think I'll ask them, if I ever see them again."

"M.B., they don't want to hear your brilliant interpretations of things."

"Who cares?" Mary Beth came back. "Those guys wouldn't pay attention to me if I were handing out free tickets to a Springsteen concert." She leaned back on the rock and fluffed her bangs, which were turning the color of copper wire.

"Don't start, you two," begged Carrie. Mary Beth had become more and more talkative as the week had gone by, and it grew hotter and more close. And the more Mary Beth expressed herself, the more Zane seemed to resent it. "It's too hot."

They called a truce, sprawling across what Zane called their "tanning" rocks and M.B. called their "burning" rocks. Zane posed in her leopard print bikini with one knee cocked, her earring glistening against her brown, shiny neck. Mary Beth pulled a damp T-shirt over her one-piece Speedo.

"Is it time yet?" Mary Beth asked, after a few minutes of silently staring down at the river.

Every twenty minutes or so, Carrie would yell "Time!" and the girls would plunge into the icy water. That was the best system they'd devised for keeping cool.

Carrie didn't respond. She was peering back at the brush behind the big rocks, down the dirt trail that wound around a small horse corral and finally ended up a few blocks off Main Street.

"I just wish I knew if Daryl was still here or not," Zane answered instead.

"He probably left, Zane."

"But summer just started."

"Zane, forget it."

"I knew that first night was my only chance. I knew I would never see him again. I knew it."

"Zane, maybe Daryl just went back to the city during the week. Maybe he and his friends only come down on weekends. Maybe he'll be back, now that it's Friday."

Zane sat up and looked back out across the river. Suddenly she threw back her hair and gasped. "That's it. Of course, that's it! He goes back during the week. And he'll be back here tonight. So we'd better sneak downtown again tonight!"

"Zane," Mary Beth moaned and held her stomach.

"We will sneak out," Zane said, as if the issue were totally decided.

Carrie's attention had been recaptured. She was no longer staring back at the trail. "I don't know. I can't believe we haven't been caught yet. Maybe we shouldn't push it."

"We won't get caught. We have it all figured out. It's totally safe now."

Carrie cringed. "I can't figure out if it's getting safer or more dangerous."

They'd snuck out twice since that first night. In fact, it was now so practiced that it had a name — "sneak attack." They mentioned that name often in hushed giggles and secret asides. They'd learned exactly what the best time was to leave so that they could escape undetected and return after the lights were out. They hadn't stayed out for more than an hour, and hadn't come in much after one. Both times Melvin had barked like crazy, but Melvin always seemed to bark, so no one was suspicious.

"Not tonight," Carrie decided.

"Why? Nothing bad ever happens," Zane moaned.

When Zane pouted, Mary Beth pinched her. "If they're in town, we'll see them at the dance tomorrow. And if we're going to go to that dance, we'll need our beauty rest."

Zane made her Godzilla face and finally, they all laughed. As far as Zane was concerned, the last two sneak attacks hadn't really counted. The second time they'd snuck out had been on Monday night, which turned out to be such a dead night downtown that even The Sweet Shoppe had closed at six. So they paced up and down Main Street, bolstering Mary Beth and pigging out on frozen bananas. They ended up getting so bored that they sang old camp songs and told junior high secrets on the dark journey home.

The third sneak attack, on Wednesday, had been a little more like the first. Zane had raced down to the boat dock first thing. But this time she was unsuccessful in finding Daryl. Daryl and his red motorboat seemed to have disappeared. Mary Beth had refused to join Zane and ended up in the roller rink by herself. And Carrie had wandered off by her mysterious self, although Mary Beth had trailed her long enough to know that Carrie had gone to The Sweet Shoppe.

Carrie *had* gone to see Phillip again, Wednesday night, after The Sweet Shoppe had closed up, leaving the two of them undisturbed. Over the hum of the big silver freezers and beneath the soft clip of the overhead fan, Carrie had sung him the first part of her new song, which was called, "Listen to the River." Phillip had explained to her how he collected apple tree branches and was going to graft two different trees together, so that he'd have a tree that bore green and red apples in the same year. When it was time to go, they'd stared at each other again and stood close, not moving, until Carrie felt as heady as if she were shooting a giant rapid.

In the two days since, Phillip had met her on his lunch breaks. She'd arranged an elaborate system where he waited for her next to the horse corral behind Mueller's Bend. His signal was a call that sounded halfway between a flute and a whistle. She pretended that it was part of their listening game, but in reality it was to keep Phillip away from Zane. He'd mentioned the college boys again, saying how furious he was about their leaky gas tank and their attitude. And Carrie knew that in Phillip's eyes Zane was probably guilty as well.

But it was all going by in such an overheated blur, that it was hard to think about things logically. Phillip was terrifically busy getting ready for the Fourth, and there was always a breathless, electric quality to their meetings that made more mundane trains of thought impossible.

Everyone was feeling the heat. Carrie's dad was too busy to take them water skiing more than once. Leslie was still around, her wet towel always hanging on the clothesline she'd stretched between the sofa and the porch rail. It was beginning to feel as if they were all cooped up together in this too hot, too intense, too confusing land of boats and water and bright summer sun.

Carrie glanced back up at the trail. She saw nothing but boulders, mounds of scrub oak, and a wild rose past its bloom. She listened for Phillip's call but heard only the sweep of the river and Zane's antsy shifting. Carrie told herself not to think so much about Phillip right now. This was the biggest weekend at The Sweet Shoppe. Between the dance and the fireworks, Watson River was going to be packed with tourists. Phillip had warned her that he would be working every minute, dishing out ice cream and sodas and fresh peach shakes. She had to make the hours move faster until the holiday was past, and she could see Phillip again. "TIME!" she announced.

Zane groaned and squinted harder across the river. "I wonder how long it takes to drive here from Pacific Heights."

Carrie put one hand out to M.B. and the other out to Zane. "Triple dive on my count." She pulled Zane's arm.

Zane stood up reluctantly, but Mary Beth popped to her feet. "Okay. Triple," Mary Beth repeated.

"M.B.," moaned Zane, "I just put more cocoa butter on."

Mary Beth and Carrie exchanged glances. Carrie placed her arms in an inverted "V" above her head, preparing for a graceful dive. Mary Beth pinched her nose. Zane tried to sit back down.

Before another word could be said, Carrie was counting. "One, two, three . . ."

Carrie dove off the rock. Then Mary Beth pulled Zane up and shoved her. "AHHHAHHHAHHHH!!!!!!!!" Mary Beth yodeled like in some old Tarzan movie.

And all three of them were in the air, falling straight toward the water.

By five they were shuffling back to the house. There had been some misunderstanding about when Carrie's dad was picking them up. But that had happened before, so they took off, drooping in the dry heat. Mary Beth had a big sun hat on and a towel wrapped around her waist. The towel didn't want to stay wrapped, and her thongs were picking up gravel from the road. She couldn't walk as fast as Carrie and Zane, but she didn't mind walking behind. She was sick of hearing about Daryl and his stupid red boat. She was sick of Zane deluding herself about some college boy. If there was one thing Mary Beth was not into, it was delusions.

On the other hand, Carrie was wandering around in a state of altered reality. Mary Beth figured that it had to do with Phillip Davison, but she couldn't be completely sure. She'd tried to ask Carrie. But Carrie merely reacted with smiles and shrugs. Mary Beth was getting tired of the way Carrie pretended that nothing weird was going on. Between the sneak attacks and the way Carrie wandered off from Mueller's Bend, Mary Beth knew that something was up.

M.B. shuddered when she thought about the sneak attacks. Sure, it was getting easier, but she still got that army-blanket feeling in her stomach. She told herself that they would be heading back to L.A. soon, so she shouldn't make a big deal out of it. And yet, she could feel trouble, she could smell it. Maybe it made her overly cautious and a twerp, but she couldn't help it. She had a special gift for sensing these things.

When they reached the house, they saw that the truck was gone. They quietly trudged up the wooden steps, worn out from the heat and the dusty uphill walk. There was no bark or hello when they reached the porch. As usual, the door was wide open, although the cabin looked empty.

"Anybody home?" Carrie called.

No answer. The girls pinned their towels to Leslie's clothesline. Right away Zane and Carrie headed for the bathroom. They'd worked out an arrangement where Zane would take a quick shower first, then sit in the steam and condition her hair while Carrie took her turn. A moment later, the rumble of the shower started and Mary Beth was alone on the porch. She walked over to a hammock that Carrie's dad had put up a couple of nights before. One end was tied to a beam, and the other to a fat branch that hung out over the porch.

"At last," Mary Beth sighed. She carefully lowered herself into the sling of fabric and began to rock. "A few minutes of peace." So many thoughts were swinging around her mind. That Zane was deceiving herself about Daryl. That Carrie was deceiving them about where she went on those walks at Mueller's Bend. That maybe it was okay to be homey and cautious. That she needed to confront Zane and her mother and say, "Face facts! Daryl feels the same way about you as I do about driving the freeways or declaring my major. Just face it."

She didn't realize that she was actually talking out loud to herself, until she saw two people — strangers — at the top of the wooden stairs. The couple was looking around the porch. Mary Beth had no idea how long they'd been standing there.

"Are Dan and Leslie here?"

Mary Beth jumped up, startled. The hammock swung as she giggled and gawked. The couple were a little older than Leslie. They were well tanned and dressed in cut-offs and T-shirts and hiking boots. The man had curly hair and John Lennon glasses, and the woman was wearing a Coca-Cola sun hat, the kind with just the brim and the emblem showing.

"You must be Dan's daughter," said the woman.

"No. She's in the shower."

"Are Dan and Leslie inside?"

"What?"

"Dan and Les. Are they here?"

Mary Beth shook her head. Something about the way the woman had put Carrie's father's name and Leslie's together made that scratchy feeling come back with a vengeance. Mary Beth grabbed her stomach, even though she wasn't sure why she was in such a panic.

"We were supposed to meet them on Table Mountain," the woman said. "We goofed up and got lost. We thought maybe they came back here." Her boyfriend sat at the picnic table and started to scribble a note.

135

"I don't know when Mr. Cates is coming back," Mary Beth mumbled. "Um, we just got home."

"I'm sure they didn't miss us," the man smirked. The woman frowned at him and put a finger to her lips. He didn't pick up on his girlfriend's concern. "Knowing them, they probably ditched us so they could be by themselves."

The woman cleared her throat loudly and whispered, "Ken, can it." Looking guilty, Ken folded his note and stood up. The woman took his arm and started leading him back to the stairs. "It's no big deal," she told Mary Beth.

"Just give them the note," added Ken.

"I will."

"Come on, Ken."

" 'Bye," Mary Beth said.

" 'Bye."

Mary Beth waited until they disappeared, then dropped easily into the hammock. She didn't tip or rock or sway, and yet she felt as unsteady as if she'd just ridden the Flying Teacups at Disneyland. That same feeling was making her lightheaded and queasy. She was gifted with perceptiveness, but this was a puzzle she hadn't dreamed of putting together.

Maybe she was mistaken. Pushing herself up again, she went straight for a pile of old magazines and mail, one of the piles she'd been so fascinated with that very first morning at the cabin. There were some postcards that had caught her eye, even though she hadn't been able to make sense of the messages. They were in a messy stack on the bottom shelf of a ratty old side table. On top were movie schedules and faculty notices, outdoor catalogues and advertising flyers. She sorted through the pile and found the three picture postcards she'd remembered. One had a photo of a cable car, one was a Far Side cartoon, and the third showed the cover of a 1940s romance magazine. They were covered with writing, front and back. Inside jokes. Affectionate messages. They were all addressed to Dan Cates, and they were all signed "CAN'T STAND IT 'TIL I SEE YOU AGAIN. Love, love, LOVE, Leslie."

"What are you looking at, M.B.?" Carrie asked, suddenly appearing in the doorway.

"What!" Mary Beth gasped, clapping the cards against her chest. "Nothing."

The shower had started to rumble again. Carrie strolled onto the porch and sat on Leslie's sofa. She was wearing her lacy antique bathrobe and had a towel around her hair. "The shower feels great," she told Mary Beth. "Did somebody stop by?"

Mary Beth sat frozen, the postcards still plastered against her. She didn't know how to get rid of them. "Friends of your dad's. And Leslie's."

"What did they want?"

"To find your dad. And Leslie."

"Did you tell them they weren't here?"

Mary Beth nodded. "They left a note."

"Oh." Carrie laid out on the sofa, stretching out her legs and nestling her face on her hands.

Mary Beth heard the shower stop. A moment

later, Zane was posing in the cabin doorway, wearing an electric-pink leotard and track shorts. She combed her hair, spreading the sweet smell of soap and hair conditioner.

"Both of them. Your dad and Leslie," Mary Beth repeated, knowing that she wasn't making much sense. That feeling inside was overwhelming. She felt as if she would explode all over the porch. This time she wasn't sure she could hold back. It was the truth. Reality. She sensed it, as sure as she sensed bad weather or a dangerous undertow. For once in her life, she had to say something. "Together."

"What?" Carrie looked confused.

Zane stayed in the doorway, carefully examining the ends of her hair.

"Your dad and Leslie. These people who came by, they were looking for them. Together."

"So?"

Zane huffed. "M.B., don't be such a nerd. What are you trying to say?"

A flash of anger jolted Mary Beth. "I'm trying to say . . . oh, forget it." Even though she was sure that she would tell the truth, Zane's impatience stopped her.

"What?"

Zane rolled her eyes. "Don't act like you have something to tell us and then say it's nothing."

"Well . . ."

"M.B., WHAT?"

"Just that I think Leslie is Carrie's father's girlfriend, that's all."

A short, shocked silence was filled by a bird's squall and a ruffle of hot wind.

"She is not!" Carrie scoffed, sitting up so quickly that her towel fell off her head. Her hair was wet and matted, making her eyes look enormous.

Zane slapped the doorway with her fist. "Mary Beth, you don't know what you're talking about. You never know what you're talking about. Leslie is just his student."

"No, she isn't."

"How do you know!"

Mary Beth couldn't explain how she knew. Of course there was Ken and the woman with the Coca-Cola hat and the postcards. But those bits of evidence weren't complete proof. Mary Beth just knew it, the way she always knew what grades she was going to get, which couples were going to break up at school, or when her dog was going to have puppies. It wasn't anything mystical. She just paid close enough attention to pick up the important signs.

"That's not true," insisted Carrie.

"Mary Beth," Zane threatened. She finally left her place in the doorway and went over to comfort Carrie. "You can be such a jerk sometimes."

"I'm not a jerk."

Carrie stood up. Her face was red and her mouth trembled. "It's not true. My father doesn't hide stuff from me. Besides, she's way too young for him. And if Leslie was his girlfriend, why would he act like she wasn't anyone important?"

"Yeah," Zane agreed. "M.B., you are so dumb."

"Zane, shut up."

Carrie stood there for another second, then turned and headed for the kitchen. "I don't want to talk about this anymore. Come on, Zane," she said pointedly. "Let's see if there's anything for dinner."

Zane followed swiftly, turning back only to give a scornful look at Mary Beth.

The screen door clacked shut and Mary Beth was left alone on the porch. She folded herself down on the rough plank floor and let the postcards drop into her lap. That scratchy feeling was gone, but it had been replaced by an emptiness, a loneliness so powerful that Mary Beth wished she could close her eyes and beam herself back home that very instant. She missed her mother. She missed her fish, her stereo, and her books, and the Paris wallpaper in her room. She wished with all her heart that she could turn back the clock to before she'd said such a stupid thing about Carrie's father. If only she could take it back, she'd never say anything, ever again.

Chapter 12

"WATSON RIVER CELEBRATES INDEPENDENCE DAY. JOIN US!!!"

The next day a big banner in red, white, and blue was draped across Main Street. In smaller letters it announced the activities for the Fourth, including the roller rink dance, a wine tasting, and the fireworks down at the beach. By then it seemed impossible that there was a person in the county who hadn't already heard. The previous night had been a steady explosion of firecrackers. Main Street was set up for a parade and a crafts show. What's more, the dance would be the biggest of the summer, so even if someone could ignore the flags waving, they'd have to notice the stream of people coming up to the roller rink to buy dance tickets.

But Phillip wasn't thinking about the dance or the parade. Not yet. It was early. There was still a wet, clean feel to the air as he biked down to the bluff above Mueller's Bend on his way to work. The wind soothed his face and his legs felt strong. But then he seemed to feel soothed and strong a lot this week, especially when he was on his way to meet Carrie. He turned off the road and onto the trail, maneuvering around rocks and ruts until he coasted sidesaddle and then stopped.

She was already there. Sitting on a rock, staring down at the river. Usually he had to call for her and she would show up breathless, looking behind her. He suspected that it was because she didn't want to mix him with her college friends. But today her posture looked so limp that he was hit with a wave of fear. Stan was making her leave town. She was going to tell him that she had a steady boyfriend back in L.A. and this whole thing had been a joke. She was going to explain that she was just like her friend with the pink-streaked hair. She wanted boys with motorboats and cars, not a soda jerk who liked to graft trees and row on the river.

"Hi," he said, propping his bike against a tree.

She barely answered. She was holding her guitar, but not playing it. "Hi."

He sat down on the ground before her. She wouldn't quite meet his gaze. Her eyes looked tired, disillusioned.

"Is something wrong?"

She shrugged. "I'm just thinking about stuff."

"What stuff?"

She strummed the guitar aimlessly. "Nothing. I guess it's just hot. My friends aren't getting along with each other. That's it."

Her friends, Phillip repeated to himself. He

had this weird flash that her friends had told her not to hang out with that townie. Dump that rowboat soda jerk before your whole summer is wasted. Still, when he looked at Carrie's lovely face again, he couldn't imagine her believing that. Not after the way they talked to each other. He scooted forward, until he was kneeling right in front of her. "Did something happen, Carrie?"

She looked at him and her blue eyes searched his face, looking for some kind of answer. But he didn't know the question she was asking. For some strange reason all he could suddenly think of was reaching his hand under the back of her hair and kissing her. It was something he'd been thinking about a lot lately. It was also a thought so startling and so nerve-wracking that he stood up and took a step back. "What's new with your father?" he said, changing the subject as firmly as he could.

Carrie's head jolted up. "Nothing," she answered in a voice that was almost angry. She kicked a stone across the ground.

"Oh." Phillip was totally confused now. "Okay."

They stayed there for what must have been five minutes while Carrie plucked her guitar and Phillip watched her. Finally, when he couldn't stay a moment longer, he reminded her, "Carrie, I have to go and start setting up the store. I don't know if I'll be able to see you much today." He picked up his bike and started back down the trail.

"Phillip!"

He turned back. His eyes locked onto hers and once again he was sure that everything between them was still the same.

"I'm sorry I'm so weird. I'll explain later. I can't quite talk about it yet. Will I see you at the dance?"

"I don't know. I'll try to get away, but I don't know."

" 'Bye."

" 'Bye."

She went back to her guitar and Phillip climbed on his bike.

With each push of his legs, he got a tight, edgy feeling. He carried that feeling with him for the whole day while he rolled cones, baked candy, set up the counter, and made ice cream cakes. He was insanely busy, and yet he kept thinking about her. He kept mulling over the awful possibility that she was just some sixteen-year-old summer person setting him up for a fall.

"It's not true," Phillip mumbled as he pounded the cash register and made change for two boys who left boasting about their chances of meeting good-looking girls over at the rink.

It was getting dark. There had been a lull before the night's activities during which the dance band did their sound check and Phillip washed glasses and refilled the syrup dispensers. He even put on the dopey red, white, and blue apron his father wanted him to wear. But now people were on the streets again. There were hoots and raucous laughs and the shrill whistle of roman candles. The band next door was well into their first set and the dance patrons' cars were already double-parked in The Sweet Shoppe lot, even though Phillip's father had put up a sign asking them to leave it clear.

Phillip's dad was due back soon from his dinner break. Then the night would take off with its own crazy rhythm. Usually on holiday nights, the pace built steadily, reaching a wild pitch somewhere before eleven. But when Phillip looked out the window again, his heart took such a set of leaps that it could have been the height of a five-hour rush.

Carrie was out there! Lingering in front of the shop window. She wore a loose antique dress that was pale yellow, cinched at the waist with a lavender scarf. Usually she didn't do anything fancy with her hair, but tonight she had one side pulled back in a tiny French braid. She lifted her hand in a limp wave but did not smile.

Phillip wanted to run around the counter, to wave his arms and yell, "Save one dance for me. Somehow I'll get over to the rink, even if I have to leave the shop during the height of the rush." But then he looked more closely. The girl with the pink-streaked hair was tugging at Carrie, chattering energetically and leaning close. Phillip looked for Carrie's other friend, the young-looking redhead. She stood separately, next to the curb, leaning sullenly on a parked car.

Phillip was halfway around the counter. He didn't want to deal with Carrie's friend, especially if her college boyfriends were lurking nearby. But for Carrie's sake, he'd at least appear in the doorway to say hello. Now that he looked at Carrie's posture under the harsh street lamps he got the feeling that there might really be something wrong — Carrie probably hadn't been trying to dump him this morning at all. She was bound to explain when they could finally find a quiet moment.

"Carrie," he called in a soft voice.

Carrie didn't hear him. He was in front of the counter now, reaching for the door. The bell jangled. But before Phillip could stick his head out, a chubby girl wiggled by him and bounded into the shop.

"Hey, great apron," she snickered as she flopped over the counter. A boy in a jean jacket dashed in after her. He grabbed the girl's round hips. They began to giggle and neck.

Phillip looked down at his apron and cringed. "What can I get for you?" he managed to ask. He let the door swing shut and backed over to the counter. When he looked up again, Carrie and her friends were gone.

The band was called Jay and the Rockers and they played a blasting, country rock that made Zane's limbs feel like they were flowing with molten lava. She wore huggy spandex pants and a pink tube top. Her hair was shiny and fragrant over her bronzy shoulders, and even though she'd had to check her high heels to protect the wooden floor, she knew she looked good.

"WA-HOOOOOOO!!!" she screamed to the ceiling, which was braided with red, white, and blue streamers. The music was so loud that Zane couldn't hear herself, but could only feel the scrape of her voice against her throat. "Finally, something is happening!"

"Zane, where are we going?" Carrie asked, grabbing Zane and yelling in her ear.

Zane stopped and looked behind her. A strobe flashed camouflage patterns on people's bodies. She could barely see her own legs, let alone the benches along the rink wall or the rail that surrounded the skating floor. About the only thing she could focus on clearly was the band platform and the musicians in their Hawaiian shirts and Day-Glo ties. "I'm trying to figure out who's here. It's not easy."

"Where's Mary Beth?"

"I don't know." Zane stepped down onto the dance floor. Dragging Carrie behind her, she zig-zagged through groups of boys hanging out by the rail. Boys who smiled. Boys who stared. Even a few boys who wouldn't look at them. Zane continued to tour the floor. The music throbbed. The rink smelled of wood and sweat. She was bumped by backs and shoulders, and twice someone stepped on her bare feet.

"We shouldn't leave M.B. alone. Not here."

"Mary Beth can be on her own for one night, Carrie. It's good for her." Zane had ditched Mary Beth as soon as they'd handed in their tickets. She knew that M.B. was probably standing in some corner, feeling awkward and left behind. But for once she didn't want to think about what Mary Beth said or sensed or observed. For once

Zane didn't want to see that oh-so-smart look in Mary Beth's eyes. For once, Zane didn't want to deal with Mary Beth, period.

"Oh, my God." Zane thrust a hand out, as if they were in danger of stumbling over the edge of a cliff. Lightning zapped through her as her eyes snapped open. She threw herself against Carrie, hugging her. Zane told herself that she was wrong. All week she kept thinking she saw Daryl. In the boat store. At the gas station. On the bridge. Then she would look again and it would be a fourteen-year-old or some guy who wasn't even blond. She wanted to see him so badly that she saw him whether he was really there or not. Surely, it was happening again.

Carrie was peeling Zane away from her. The music ended with a big finish and when it was a little quieter she said, "Is that Daryl, Zane? Is that him?"

Zane lifted her head. Three boys were approaching the band platform, checking out the group's equipment. The trio was clearly lit by the spill from Jay and the Rockers' spotlights. There was no denying it. Justin, with his pug face and beefy body. Matt, still wearing his mirrored glasses even though you could barely see your own feet. And Daryl, looking softer, younger, blonder, and handsomer than his two friends.

"It's him! I knew he'd come back. I knew it."

Carrie shrugged.

Zane gripped Carrie's wrist. She started across the floor. "Come with me."

"Zane, you go ahead." Carrie tugged in the direction of the exit. "Maybe I'll go outside and get some air."

Zane held onto Carrie with such ferociousness that she startled even herself. She made such a big deal about Mary Beth being a chicken, and yet she was suddenly stunned into panic. Meeting the boys on the dock had been one thing. Even asking to ride on their boat after dark hadn't unnerved her. Somehow she had known that nothing was really going to happen. Nothing ever *really* happened. But this was a dance. It was dark and the band had just launched into a slow song. Couples wove their arms around each other's waists. Some barely moved. A few kissed and reached under the backs of sweaters and shirts. "You have to come with me!"

"I don't even know them."

"Come on!" Before Carrie could protest again, Zane was dragging her over to the band platform.

Zane pushed her way through groping couples, groups of teenagers trying to look like they didn't mind not dancing, and two college girls dancing a silly swing with each other. Carrie, who didn't seem very interested in either the music or the dancers, finally decided to follow.

Zane moved closer until she felt the band spotlight warm her skin. The hot light hit her face and Daryl finally looked right at her. For a second there was nothing in his eyes. No joy. No disdain. Not even recognition. Then Justin slapped his back and said something. The three boys laughed and Daryl took a step away from the platform and toward Zane.

"It's Olive Oyl, right?" He approached Zane with his hands on his hips. He wore white jeans, a dark untucked polo shirt, and loafers with no socks. His hair looked almost golden under the bright band light.

Zane stepped closer and was overpowered by a cologne that smelled of lime and grass. "Hi." Carrie sat aimlessly on the edge of the band platform. "This is my friend Carrie."

Daryl tipped his chin in Carrie's direction. His two buddies were back checking out Jay's Fender amp.

"So, Olive," Daryl said, looking back in Zane's eyes. "Do you want to dance?"

Zane's knees went loose. "Sure." She shrugged, trying to appear semi-cool. She gave a quick glance back at Carrie as Daryl led her onto the floor.

Soon they were swallowed up by a crowd of barely moving bodies. Daryl slipped his hands around Zane's waist and pulled her in. She laced her arms around his shoulders. Her cheek was next to the bare skin of his neck, which was hot, like a day in the sun. They began to move in slow motion. Zane was glad that he kept squeezing her more and more tightly. Because if he let go she was afraid she would melt right into the middle of the roller rink floor.

Late.

Nearly eleven. Carrie sat on the curb at the

corner and stared down at the beach. Fireworks were shooting into the sky. Bugs fluttered around. Phillip had told her about a bat that lived by the river and twisted and turned down Main Street, scaring tourists half to death. Except tonight it was more likely that the bat would be scared. Kids were screaming and waving sparklers. The smoke curled around their heads and left halos. Main Street was littered with the refuse from the M-80s, the dive bombers, and sputterers, the carefully hoarded arsenal of crackers, smokebombs, and rockets saved for this night.

"Let's hear it for Jay and the Rockers!" blared an overmiked voice from inside the roller rink. "If you yell loud enough, maybe they'll play a few more songs. All together now . . ."

"YEAAAHHHHHHHHHHH!!!"

Carrie covered her ears. She felt anything but together. Actually, she felt as if she were splitting into pieces. Maybe it was the heat. Maybe it was cabin fever. Maybe it was that she, Zane, and Mary Beth — the trio so famous at Sherman High — were about as united tonight as aliens from three different planets. It had been that way since last night.

Maybe it was that weird stuff that Mary Beth had said about Leslie and her father — even though Carrie knew that it wasn't true and wasn't sure that it should matter if it *were* true. But the thought that it might be true made Carrie want to throw things and race for the next plane home. Since last night, Carrie had watched her father carefully, looking for signs and hints.

But he was the same as ever. Cheerful. Busy. Not paying a lot of attention to Leslie. Giving Carrie a hug and a smile, but not sticking around long enough for her to probe into anything too serious.

Maybe it was that she hadn't been able to talk to Phillip that morning, when she'd been so gloomy and preoccupied. She'd wanted to tell him about what Mary Beth had said about her father. But how could she tell him, especially when it wasn't, couldn't possibly be true! And they hadn't been able to get together since. He hadn't snuck over to the rink for a single dance.

After finally leaving the roller rink, Carrie had walked by The Sweet Shoppe two more times, hoping that Phillip would come out and talk to her. But he was wildly busy. Sure, he'd warned her that on the Fourth the shop did its best business of the entire summer, but she wanted him to read her mind. So she'd stood in the parking lot while he spun from the milkshake machine to the ice cream freezers, from the soda dispenser to the register. He'd replaced a dropped cone, thrown away two broken glasses, and she'd read his lips when he asked someone not to smoke. Customers poured in and out. Some yelled at him, some joked, some asked for directions. Phillip didn't have time to notice her at all.

Carrie had spent the last half hour sitting on the curb in front of the boat shop. Even though she could hear the music, the noise of the street, and the ooohs following each firework as it de-

scended down onto the beach, she felt empty.
Alone. Not the stifled, stuck feeling she had with
Stan, but something much scarier. A lonely, hollow feeling that everything wonderful was about
to disappear. It was a feeling that paralyzed her.
It made her want to hug herself, to crawl back
into her sleeping bag, to close her eyes and not
have to deal with being sixteen ever again.

She was incredibly relieved to finally spot a
slim, auburn-haired girl plodding slowly up from
the direction of the beach. Mary Beth offered a
halfhearted wave. When Carrie waved back,
M.B. shuffled over and sat next to her.

"Hi, M.B.," Carrie muttered.

Mary Beth chewed on her thumbnail. "You left
the dance, too?"

"Too loud."

"I stayed for about five minutes. I have this
instinct for figuring things out — like that no one
was going to ask me to dance. So I left right
away." Mary Beth put her face in her hands. "Oh.
Never mind." She stretched her legs out in front
of her. For the dance she'd dressed up in a jade-
green pullover and her best blue jeans. "I'm
sorry. I should just shut up."

"It's okay."

"No it isn't." Mary Beth looked around.
"Where's Zane?"

"She found that guy."

"Popeye?"

Carrie nodded. "When I left she was dancing
with him. Well, sort of dancing. More like just

standing there grabbing each other."

"I just hope she remembers that your dad is picking us up at eleven-thirty."

Carrie looked down in the direction of the river. "She will." A green, yellow, and red pom-pom had just exploded with shrieks and pops. It flashed colored light onto the side of The Sweet Shoppe. Carrie stared at the ice cream parlor.

"You like him, don't you?" Mary Beth blurted. "Phillip, I mean." As soon as she said it, she shook her head furiously, as if she wished she could take the words back.

"Yes, I do," Carrie answered simply. "A lot."

"I'm sorry I said that. I didn't mean anything, I just . . ."

"It's okay, M.B. Honest."

They watched a triple explosion of red, white, and blue burst in the sky and sweep down. A long, amazed AHHHHH drifted up from the shore.

"Do you want to go over and see him?"

Carrie didn't budge. "He didn't show up at the dance at all. When I ran into him this morning, it was pretty weird."

"Oh."

Carrie looked at Mary Beth. Her friend's face had changed over the last two weeks. It was getting a tanned, angular look that was starting to make her look like those girls who ran for class office or won poetry contests. "Do you think I should? Maybe I should go over and talk to him."

Mary Beth started to answer, then shook her head. "Don't ask me for advice."

Carrie suddenly stood up. She'd never been hesitant with Phillip before and yet, after hearing Mary Beth's comment about her father, she was less sure of everything in the world. Still, she told herself that morning had been weird because she was thinking about her father and Leslie. "Come on. Let's get an ice cream. At least we should do one fun thing tonight."

"Okay."

They jogged across the street, and Carrie saw at once that the crowd inside The Sweet Shoppe had thinned out. There were only about five people waiting at the counter and Phillip's dad was carrying a stack of boxes into the back room. They went in and the bell on the door jangled.

Phillip looked up at once. His apron was spattered like a painting by Jackson Pollock and he looked tired. Even so, the corners of his mouth started to lift and those two dimples began to sink into his cheeks. His dark hair was shiny under the harsh shop lights and his green eyes were focused only on Carrie.

"Hi," Carrie said. Her limbs felt warm and buzzy. His smile was wiping out her doubt. "Oh, this is Mary Beth. M.B., this is Phillip."

They smiled at one another.

"It's not so busy now," Carrie offered.

"Finally." For a moment Phillip just gazed at her.

"Has it really been bad? I've been wanting to talk to you, to tell you what's been . . ."

"I tried to get away, but it's been a zoo."

Just then the shop door swung open with a

loud, repeating *clang*. Phillip flinched as if he'd been hit with an electric shock. Half a dozen loud voices thrust themselves into the shop. Carrie was confused at first. But then she whipped around to see Daryl and Zane with their arms wrapped around each other. Daryl's two pals were with them, and so were two college girls.

"Here you are, Carrie! Where've you been?" Zane said, unraveling herself from Daryl and making her way across the floor to join Carrie. She grinned and dangled her high heels in one hand. Daryl stayed in the doorway with his friends and the other girls.

Phillip threw a wet cloth down on the counter, wiping the same square foot over and over and over. He pretended not to notice Zane, or Daryl, or Daryl's friends. And yet, Carrie knew that he was hyper aware of all of them.

"I left early," Carrie told Zane.

Zane finally spotted Mary Beth. She flinched and her mouth tightened. "Oh, hi, M.B." She posed with her back to the counter and Phillip, her brown elbows perched on the ledge. "Guess what!"

"What?"

Zane flung her head back. Her shoes were practically on the counter. Carrie could see Phillip cringe as Zane moved closer to her and said in a loud voice, "I told Daryl about our sneak attacks and he wants us to come back down here tonight so he can take us out on his boat. He promised he'd wait for us. He'll even take all of us." She gave Mary Beth a forgiving smile.

"Even you, M.B." Then she fell against the counter in a mock faint. Her shoes almost hit Phillip. "Carrie, I have been having the most amazing night."

Mary Beth settled onto a stool and pretended to be fascinated with the ceiling fan.

"Zane," Carrie said, aware that Phillip was standing very close, bent over the counter with the wet rag in one hand. "This is Phillip." Phillip didn't raise his head. "Remember him? I think you talked to each other the first day we were here."

Zane glanced back at Daryl and his friends. She looked nervous suddenly, as if they might run off without her. Then, for a split second, she lost that wild-eyed fervor and was the old, kooky Zane. "Hi, Phillip. Happy Fourth," she said in a neutral voice, a voice that gave Carrie hope.

Carrie touched Zane's arm. "I know you weren't really thinking the first time you and Phillip met. I thought if you gave each other another . . ."

She didn't finish because an ear-splitting laugh cut her off. A moment later Daryl had joined them. He draped himself over Zane. "So, are you going to join us, do your sneak out attack, or whatever you call it?" He noticed that Phillip was glaring at him. "Hey. If it isn't the soda jerk!" He winked at Phillip.

Zane leaned into Daryl as he tickled her, causing her tube top to creep up. "Daryl. This is Phillip." She flopped back over the counter. "Phillip, this is Daryl. A friend of mine. And

Carrie's." She nudged Carrie. "And Mary Beth's." When Mary Beth didn't react, Zane stuck her tongue out.

Carrie saw the tiredness in Phillip's face harden like plaster. He backed away from the counter, as Matt, Justin, and the college girls started to yell from the doorway.

"I thought we came here to get something to eat," one of the girls whined.

"Maybe he has a leaky ice cream freezer," whined Matt.

"Yeah, it might leak on the floor and kill the cockroaches."

"You'd better get it fixed, Davison, or we'll report you!"

Zane looked as mortified as Carrie. For a moment Daryl looked tense, too, but then he shouted as well, "We won't hold it against you, okay? We'll just take four thousand banana splits. Hold the whipped cream on three of them."

When Daryl joined in, Zane hopped onto a stool. "Well, what does everybody want?" she asked in a voice that was too loud and falsely cocky. She leaned over and gave Phillip a flirty smile. "Is it all on the house?"

"Give me a break," Phillip grumbled under his breath.

"What did you say, jerk?" Daryl laughed.

"I said get lost."

Just then Phillip's dad came out from the back. Carrie saw him frown and then he came up to the counter. "Phillip, have these people been served?"

"No, we haven't," Daryl said in an overly proper voice. All the college kids snickered.

"Well, let's get on it," Mr. Davison said.

Carrie cringed inside. She could see the humiliation on Phillip's face. She held her breath waiting to see if the tension would explode and there would be a scene. But under the imposing gaze of his father, Phillip pulled it back in. He reached for a scoop and became like a robot. "What would you like?" was all he said to Zane.

"Oil Slick Sundae."

"Maple Syrup Ripple."

"Berry Berry."

Carrie didn't know what to do. Phillip's face was turning harder and harder and even his father was looking angry and confused. She wasn't sure how to stop what was going on, and she could tell that Phillip hated having her witness it. So she grabbed Mary Beth's wrist. "Let's go, M.B." She would wait outside until Daryl and his stupid friends had gone, and then she would go back in and talk to Phillip alone. It would be better if he handled this on his own.

"Okay," Mary Beth said, standing up and starting to move.

But then Carrie saw Justin pull a book of matches out of his pocket. She knew there was no smoking and was about to say so, to save Phillip from having to make a big deal of it. That's when she realized that Justin didn't have a cigarette in his hand. Instead he held a long, gray cylinder with a papery stem. Justin was hiding it from Phillip and his dad, while he brought a match to it. There was a sparkle and a *whifft* of smoke, and the next thing Carrie saw was Justin reaching over the counter and dropping it into one of the big cartons of ice cream. She opened her mouth to warn Phillip when the explosion came.

BANG!

The firecracker went off with a tremendous crack. Carrie and Zane both screamed at the same time. People walking in the door jumped. Phillip dropped his scoop and his father whirled around. The ringing in everybody's ears stayed for several seconds. But then Carrie realized that all the college kids were laughing. As Mr. Davison walked over to the demolished barrel of splattered ice cream and shredded cardboard, his face went red with fury.

"All right," he said in a cold voice. He pointed at the boys. "All of you, out of here."

The college guys started running out. They were still howling with laughter. Finally, Zane started laughing, too. Following Daryl, she pulled on Carrie's arm. "Come on."

Carrie wasn't going. She wasn't leaving Phillip. Not now. But when she tried to look at him, his expression was as cold as his father's. He stood behind the counter, staring at the mess. Then Carrie realized that Mr. Davison was still pointing, only now it was just at her. "You heard me. Get out. You're lucky I don't call the cops on you and your friends."

"But I didn't . . . They're not my . . ."

"Out."

Carrie waited for Phillip to defend her, but he didn't even turn around. Instead he began picking up pieces of cardboard.

"OUT!" Mr. Davison yelled.

Carrie and Mary Beth ran out of the shop.

Chapter 13

"SHHHHH!"

Zane slapped a finger to her lips and spread the alarm. Melvin was barking in the hall, just outside the cabin bedroom. A crease of light had crept under the doorway and cut across their sleeping bags. Mary Beth slithered down like a worm and pulled the flannel over her head.

"Mel, what's your problem?" Carrie's father's voice came through the door. "Let the girls sleep."

"It's the fireworks," Leslie called in a loud whisper from the far end of the living room. "They freaked him out. All the dogs have been crazy today. Come on, Mel, come over here with me."

Melvin's paws clickity-clacked away and the hall light went out again. Mary Beth popped her head out.

Zane was standing at the open window. She was still in her spandex pants and tube top. She'd tied a sweater around her waist and replaced her heels with a pair of red Reeboks. "I'm going. Who's coming with me?"

Mary Beth clutched the top of her sleeping bag. Since the firecracker in The Sweet Shoppe they'd barely spoken. The whole way home with Mr. Cates they'd sat in the truck like statues. Their silence was so obvious that when they went through the motions of getting ready for bed, Mr. Cates had even commented on it.

Zane was inching back the curtain and peering out onto the porch. A glow of moonlight floated in. But other than the crickets and soft music in the living room, it was quiet. "If you're coming, let's go," she said.

Carrie was sitting up next to Mary Beth. She was still in her dress, although her hair, so carefully arranged for the dance, now streamed messily around her face. She'd never bothered to crawl into her sleeping bag. Actually, Mary Beth was the only one who'd even changed her clothes.

Suddenly Carrie pounded the bed, then stood up. "I have to go back downtown, too," she said in a determined whisper.

Zane threw a quick, dismissing glance back at Mary Beth. "Good. Then let's hit it."

"Let me just put something warmer on."

"Hurry."

Mary Beth clutched her sleeping bag while Carrie opened a drawer in slow motion and pulled one of her father's sweatshirts on over her dress. Then Carrie sat on the floor to tug on heavy socks. She began to search under the bed for one of her boots.

"Hurry!" Zane urged. "I don't know how long Daryl will wait."

Carrie moved a little faster, but Mary Beth sat as still as a slug. She felt like the invisible girl. The outcast. She knew that Carrie wasn't really mad at her anymore, and yet this whole sneak attack was going on without any acknowledgment of her. It was as if her two best friends were saying, "Fine, Mary Beth. Open your mouth and say whatever awful thing comes into your head. But when it comes to real action, we know that you're just a wimp. A twerp. So we won't even bother to include you. You just stay here — hiding in your cocoon of a sleeping bag — until we come back."

Mary Beth stared at Carrie, hoping to get some kind of reassurance. But there was nothing except for Carrie's single-minded dressing, and this enforced silence, as if they were in detention or the library. Finally Carrie found her boot and stood up. The closer she moved to Zane and the window, the more Mary Beth felt that she was being exiled. Exiled for her perceptive brain and her big mouth. Exiled from the two people she'd been closest to since seventh grade.

But Mary Beth had spoiled it — spoiled it with her big, smart mouth. Maybe taking action was a better tactic. That's what her mother always said, and maybe she was right. After all, M.B. was heading back to L.A. in a few days. Maybe she should stop thinking and talking, and instead ride red motorboats, stay at dances, and join in in what might be their last sneak attack.

"Wait," she blurted out, unzipping her bag and throwing it to one side. "I'm coming, too."

Zane stood still at the window, her posture showing her suspicion and impatience. "Okay," she finally said. "Just hurry up."

"Come on, M.B.," Carrie added. "Don't make any noise."

"I won't." But the minute she got off the bed, Mary Beth slammed into Zane's suitcase and knocked it over.

"SHHH!"

Not looking at her friends, M.B. changed her clothes so fast that it wasn't until she was out the window and on the porch that she realized she was wearing Zane's sweater. It kept falling off her shoulder no matter how many times she tugged it back up.

"Not a sound," Carrie mouthed.

The air had cooled from hot to warm. Stars were peeking out everywhere. There was a slight smokey smell and almost no wind. The lights were still on in the living room, and Melvin bayed as soon as they stepped onto the porch. But as they tiptoed down the wooden steps, the howling faded away. When they reached the road there was just the moon, the still, warm night, the lonely truck with its fat, round bumpers, and the careful crunch of gravel under their feet.

"I told Daryl I'd meet him at the boat dock," Zane said, taking off down the hill. She set the pace, moving as fast as if they were doing competitive walking. Carrie had no trouble keeping up, but Mary Beth had to trot in double time.

At the beginning of Main Street, where the Mobil station stood next to the first streetlight, Carrie finally halted. "I'm going off on my own," she said in a rushed voice. "I'll meet you back at the house." Staring straight at Zane, she warned, "Be home by one-thirty at the absolute latest. Don't you dare be a minute later than that!"

"Don't worry, Carrie. I won't. Where are you going?" Zane demanded.

Mary Beth knew Carrie's destination, but this time she kept her knowledge to herself. Her stomach had taken a sudden dive when she realized that she was going to be alone with Zane. Maybe she wasn't so perceptive after all. She hadn't predicted that she would have to be down here again without Carrie to temper Zane's wildness. She took a deep breath and tried to will the old scratchy feeling away.

Carrie had already set off down Main Street, so full of purpose that she might have been on a treasure hunt. Mary Beth stood staring after her until Zane grabbed her arm and began to run in the opposite direction. After two dark blocks and that creepy dip under the bridge, they were there. But as soon as Mary Beth heard the loud, choppy laughter of Daryl and his friends and saw that red boat waiting at the dock, she sensed that coming down here again was a huge, horrible mistake.

Zane steered her across the parking lot and over to where the boys were gathered at the dock. Only one of the college girls was still with them. She had a dark bushy ponytail and hung all over Matt, who had finally taken off his mir-rored sunglasses.

"We're here," Zane announced in a tentative voice.

Daryl jumped up and down on the dock and applauded. "Hey, you made it!" Right away, he went back to rigging something on the boat. His eyes were a little red, which made him look less handsome than Mary Beth remembered.

"*Wooooooo*," screamed Justin from inside the boat. "We're going to party tonight." The differ-ence in his demeanor was much more obvious. His cocky assurance was gone. Instead he swayed and lurched. When he saw Mary Beth he grinned. "How you doing?"

Mary Beth was so flabbergasted that he'd ac-tually spoken to her, no words would come out of her mouth. Zane stepped forward to pick up the slack. "This is my friend Mary Beth. Re-member, you said I could bring other people. I hope it's okay."

"Okay?"Justin laughed in a way that made Mary Beth want to sink into the asphalt. "The more the merrier." He flopped over and turned a boom box on full blast. A Huey Lewis number came out of the speakers and Justin started danc-ing and singing along. That was when Mary Beth saw the beer can practically attached to his hand. He pumped his arms in a way that reminded her of King Kong and drank gulp after gulp. Finally he crumpled the can in one hand, tossed it into the river, and plucked a new one from a case inside the boat.

Now that Mary Beth looked more carefully she saw that Matt and the college girl were drinking, too . . . that is, when they stopped kissing long enough to come up for sips. She grabbed Zane's hand and started to back away. She'd never been presented with this situation before, but she'd certainly seen enough of those "don't drink and drive" commercials to know how risky it was. What's more, her mother lectured her about not riding with drunks, as much as she did about what would happen when Mary Beth turned sixteen. Mary Beth decided that when it came to driving drunk, a boat and a car probably qualified as the same thing.

"Zane, let's go back," she said in a muted voice.

Zane shook her head, as if something disgusting had just run through her hair. "WHY?"

Mary Beth pulled her away from the boys, into a shadow between two parked cars. "They're drunk. We can't go on the boat with them."

"It's just beer, Mary Beth."

"Zane!" Mary Beth stopped and took a breath. She told herself to shut up, to go along with the fun and stop being such a wimp. And yet, that feeling was getting so strong that she thought she would go insane. She couldn't hold herself back. "You can get plenty drunk on beer," she blurted out. "Don't be an idiot, Zane!"

A split second of doubt fluttered across Zane's dark eyes. "Daryl's not drunk. It's just the other two."

"How do you know?"

Zane took a furious step into the light and called, "DARYL, ARE YOU DRUNK?"

"Who me?" he yelled back in a silly falsetto. All the boys guffawed. Then Daryl hopped onto the seats in the boat and balanced across them, bringing his finger to his nose. His legs were steady and his balance firm. "No problem, see?"

Zane turned back to Mary Beth. "See?"

Mary Beth hated this whole scene. More than anything she wished that she'd followed her instincts this one last time and stayed in her sleeping bag. "Is Daryl going to drive the boat? Or will it be the other guys?"

"Daryl."

"How do you know?"

"Mary Beth! Do you want me to ask him that, too?" Zane kicked the fender of a parked car. "What is wrong with you? Why do you have to see the bad part of everything?"

"I don't!"

The boys were singing now. All of them were in the boat, including Matt's girlfriend, who sat on his lap until she got tipped onto the floor.

"Ship's taking off," Daryl yelled. "All aboard."

Zane's expression slowly changed to one of anger. She looked hard at Mary Beth. "Don't wimp out on me, Mary Beth. Why did you come down here if you didn't want to go on the boat? Come on."

"No," Mary Beth said. Then she clapped her hand to her mouth, stunned that she had actually said it.

"What?"

"I'm not going. And you shouldn't go, either."

"What's the problem?" yelled Matt. He banged the side of the boat. "LET'S GET THIS SHOW ON THE WATER." His girlfriend giggled and giggled.

"Mary Beth, come on," Zane begged.

"I don't want to." Mary Beth suddenly felt the strong push of tears, as if all that held-back pressure of not standing up for herself was about to burst from her. "I don't want you to go, either."

"ANCHOR'S AWAY," hollered Justin. The motor rumbled to life.

"Don't worry so much," Zane threatened. She squeezed Mary Beth's wrists and started to pull her toward the boat.

Mary Beth twisted herself away. She was amazed at how badly Zane wanted her to come along and wondered if Zane might not be scared, too. "No. You heard me. I'm not going."

"ZANE," yelled Daryl, sounding impatient. "Hurry up or I'm leaving without you."

"Mary Beth, if you are such a wimp that you won't even come on this stupid boat, then I don't want to be friends with you any more. I can't take this."

"Well," Mary Beth said, biting back tears, "neither can I."

Zane stared at her for one more moment before breaking loose and running over to the boat. Mary Beth stood in the parking lot for a long time. She waited until Zane and the red motorboat were gone before she started to sob.

* * *

Carrie didn't know exactly where she was going. She'd been by The Sweet Shoppe already, but it was closed. The only lights coming from inside were the eerie ones that originated from the long freezer and were always on. Carrie had stood on the sidewalk outside the shop and counted shadows, but that was all. No Phillip, no Phillip's father, no one to ask if they had seen him or where he'd gone.

Across the street there were plenty of people. Partiers, revelers, stragglers from Fourth of July celebrations that had petered out. They sat on curbs, inside or on top of cars, or leaned against posts. They looked tired, some of them drunk. In fact some looked so out of it that Carrie knew they couldn't possibly help her find Phillip and were therefore not of the least bit of interest to her. In fact she wanted to avoid them at all costs. She could imagine one of them turning out to be a policeman asking for her ID.

Carrie was too stunned to deal with a policeman. What had happened earlier at The Sweet Shoppe still didn't seem real. Phillip couldn't possibly have thought that she was part of the stupid prank with the firecracker, yet he'd made no effort to find her after his father had thrown all of them out of the shop. Maybe he simply hadn't been able to connect with Carrie, but she couldn't quite believe that, either. Something had happened — either a fight with his dad, or a misunderstanding over Carrie's role in the prank, or possibly a reaction to how snobby Zane had been to him. But then it didn't really matter to Carrie anymore *what* it was, all she knew was that she had to find Phillip to explain to him that it was all a big mistake.

But then there was the job of picking him out of the people still on the street. It seemed a cruel irony that Carrie more than anything wanted to avoid looking most of these people in the eyes, but now she had to. Staying off the sidewalk, she walked back up the street, trying to remain inconspicuous as she looked at who was there. A couple of guys waved at her, and another one whistled. For the most part she was left alone.

When she got back to the top of the street she knew she was too alone. She suddenly missed Zane and Mary Beth and wished she hadn't been in so much of a hurry to leave them. But then where would she begin to explain things? She was having a hard enough time explaining everything to herself. Carrie was just about to go back to the roller rink when she heard a sound that made her jump. A baseball card plucking at spokes. She turned and walked toward the sound.

The sound led away from downtown, toward the river. Pretty soon she spotted Phillip pushing his bike along. There was no doubt it was Phillip. Even in the dark, the graceful walk was unmistakable. Carrie ran.

"Phillip, wait up."

The bike stopped. Phillip turned and looked. His face was caught in the glare of one of the streetlights and Carrie saw how sad he looked. It didn't ease up when she came closer. Phillip's eyes expressed no happiness at seeing her, and his hands remained pressed tightly around the handlebars.

He said nothing.

"I've been down here trying to find you," Carrie explained.

Phillip didn't react like the information was very important. The look he gave Carrie reminded her of the first time she'd seen him — it was cool, indifferent, and slightly scornful. Carrie wished there was something she could do to wipe it away. "Are you going home?" she finally said.

He started moving the bike again, as if he would get stuck in a rut if he didn't keep the tires rolling. Carrie kept pace with him and tried to pretend his reaction didn't matter.

"Can I talk to you?"

Phillip shook his head. "I don't know what about," he said in a tight voice.

"About tonight," Carrie explained. "I mean it isn't exactly what I wanted to have happen."

"No," Phillip answered, "but it was probably what I should have expected. Go back to your friends."

Neither one of them were looking at each other now, and the bike was like a nasty fence between them. Phillip's step was relentless, his eyes straight ahead. "I'm turning here," he announced. Then there was the fast click of the baseball card. This time Carrie knew she wasn't being invited to walk along. Phillip was moving away at a one-person pace.

She backed up slowly, reluctant to quit looking at him, but aware of how deeply she hurt. He disappeared into the darkness, although she could still hear the clicking of the spokes. Carrie didn't want to hear it much longer. She turned on the heels of her boots and walked back toward Main Street.

Chapter 14

Hot and cold.

Zane was being flung from one to the other. Hot from Daryl's attention when she had first joined him on the boat. He'd protected her from the night air, running his fingers along her bare arms and kissing her neck until she thought she would faint. But now she was cold. In fact she was trembling from the wind off the water. Worse was the way Daryl had decided to ignore her. That had made her feel really cold, even icy. Daryl had powwowed with his buddies, sharing jokes that Zane didn't understand, and joining in a stupid beer-chugging contest.

"ONE MORE. ONE MORE," Justin and Matt chanted. Daryl looked up at them and finally picked up another can. His friends applauded when he popped the tab. There was the sound of beer fizzing out and more macho laughter.

"Daryl," Zane called from her perch on the bow. His back was to her and his only response was the tilting of his blond head, while he downed another can.

"FIVE, FOUR, THREE, TWO . . . ALL RIGHT." Daryl stood up for a lurching bow and then Justin popped open a can for himself.

Zane shivered. They'd been on the water for fifteen or twenty minutes. She still had her sweater tied around her waist because she knew that Daryl liked the bareness of her arms and shoulders, and she'd liked the feel of his warm hands. But now goose bumps were popping out and her teeth were starting to chatter. And she had to wonder if Daryl even remembered that she was there.

"DARYL," she called again. She didn't want to betray any of the panic she was starting to feel. They were anchored in the middle of the river and every time one of them moved, the boat rocked like crazy. Zane was starting to have the most frightening visions. The boat tipping over. The guys starting the motor again and driving so wildly that they'd crash into a rock or a pier. Daryl getting horribly drunk and pushing her to go further than she'd ever been prepared to go.

"Hey, you guys," Zane begged. "Where are we?" When there was still no response, Zane dipped her hand into the water. The air was chilling down fast and the water felt like it had been iced. She thought they were near the place where they'd gone water skiing, but it was too dark to know for sure. All she could see was the water around her, the stars, and the occasional bright burst of a far-off firework. "DARYL."

Daryl didn't even flinch when she called his name again. Finally, Matt slurred, "Daryl, I think somebody wants you."

Justin started to laugh, a loose, out-of-control chuckle that chilled Zane even more. He tried to nudge Daryl with his elbow, but was so unstable that he toppled over like a fallen tree. Zane clutched the side of the boat. Matt's girlfriend howled.

Zane watched Daryl's blond head tip back as he started another can of beer. When they'd first taken off, she'd really thought he wanted to spend time with her. Now he was virtually ignoring her and seemed as eager to impress his pals as Zane was to impress him.

"Five, four, three, two, one!" Justin and Matt chanted.

Daryl stood up with a wobble and raised his arms, as if he'd just won an Olympic medal. He poured the beer into his mouth from a distance of four inches, so that some of it splashed on his face. Then he let out a thundering burp that echoed across the huge, open sky.

"That's so gross," Zane groaned.

Suddenly all three boys were lumbering over to her. The boat seesawed. Matt's girlfriend lost her balance, then curled up in the back of the boat and fell asleep.

"I think our friend here has some complaints," taunted Matt.

Justin held a frosty can of beer about two inches from Zane's nose. "Drink this. Then maybe you won't be such a pain."

Zane made a face. She needed to get back soon. She'd promised Carrie that she'd be back in her sleeping bag by one-thirty. When she'd imagined this boat ride she'd pictured a quick cruise up and down the shore, a few fabulous kisses. Nothing more than that. "No thanks."

"Aw, come on. What are you afraid of?"

"No thanks," Matt mimicked in a baby voice. Justin thought that was hysterical. He and Matt fell all over each other.

Zane carefully stood up and balanced her way over to Daryl. The way the boat shifted and swayed was starting to make her sick. "Daryl, come on," she pleaded, tugging on the tails of his polo shirt. He wobbled and fell against her. His face and back had grown clammy with sweat. "Let's head back to shore."

"Back to shore?" Matt came back. "We just got out here."

"I need to be back soon," Zane explained. "Please, Daryl."

But Daryl wasn't listening to her. He was flopped against her like an old mattress. When she shoved him away, he sagged down onto the ice chest as if his legs were made of sand. His head hung limply and he laughed to himself.

"Daryl," ordered Justin. He picked up Daryl's face by the chin, pointed at Zane, and asked, "Where did you ever find this pain-in-the-butt girl?"

Daryl tried to focus on Zane. He was having trouble keeping his eyes open. "That's Olive," he muttered.

"Daryl," Zane pleaded. "Let's go back."

Justin held out one of his beefy hands, gesturing for Zane to pipe down. "Daryl," he shouted, right in Daryl's ear, "so, how old is this girl anyway?"

"I dunno," Daryl mumbled.

"How old *are* you?" slurred Matt.

Zane stared down at her Reeboks. "Seventeen," she lied. Then she glanced up, to see if they'd believed her.

"Sure," hooted Matt. "Seventeen." He punched Daryl, who reacted with a gasp and a murmur. "You are such a cradle robber, Daryl. This girl isn't a day over sixteen, if she's even that, you turkey."

"Why don't you just take me back?"

Suddenly Justin and Matt elbowed each other. Daryl had just fallen off the ice chest and was clutching the side of the boat, as if he thought someone might pry him away and toss him into the water.

"Because we're not ready to go back yet. We just took the boat out." Matt made his way to the driver's seat, stepping over Daryl and the college girl. "We thought we might stay out all night."

Zane's breath quickened. She realized she was ready to cry. She was in over her head and had no idea how this had gotten out of her control so quickly. It was no use asking Daryl to stand up for her because he couldn't stand up, period. But she had to get back to the cabin, or risk getting Carrie in trouble and spoiling this entire vacation. Besides, the boys were on to her now. They knew she was young and scared. She wanted to get away from them as soon as she could.

She scooted over to one of the side benches and looked out at the water as Justin pulled the anchor in and Matt started the engine. Cold water and a string of slimy algae flicked onto Zane's arm. The smell of gasoline made her head spin and she wondered what it would be like to swim in the dark river. The more she thought about swimming through that cold, dark water, the more terrified she became. She didn't know where she was, how far away from shore, how deep the water was, or what was swimming around under the water at night.

"Just let me off, okay," she demanded, in the strongest voice she could imagine. "You don't have to go back to the main dock. Just let me off anywhere along the shore."

"You want to get off?" Justin repeated, giving her a scary smile.

"Yes!"

"Anywhere?"

"YES!"

"Okay." He howled and turned the steering wheel so abruptly that Zane thought the boat would flip over. In a minute there was the friction of land against the bottom of the bow. "Here you are. This is the only stop this bus makes."

The boys were laughing again. Zane was confused. How could they have reached shore so quickly? It had taken them at least ten minutes to get so far out into the middle of the river. She was totally disoriented and so scared that she could barely breathe.

"Everybody out," said Justin, followed by a disgusting belch.

Zane suddenly felt large hands slip under her bare arms and lift her from the boat. She started kicking her feet, but then her tube top began slipping down. So she stopped struggling and held onto her top. The next thing she knew she had been placed in cold thigh-deep water that had soaked her sweater and her pants. The boat was already gliding away from her.

"WAIT!" she screamed. "WHERE AM I?"

"You wanted off," Matt called back in a drunken howl. "What little girls want, little girls get."

Zane stood, her brain an empty screen of disbelief, until the boat was no longer in sight. Then she turned around and waded up to a barren shore. There were no docks here. No cabins. Not even an outhouse. When the sound of the motorboat had completely faded away, she realized that she was on the small island she'd seen that first day water skiing.

Zane stood trembling among the reeds and the brush. Something ran through a bush behind her, making a rustling, thumping sound. Then she felt the tickle of a moth or a mosquito against her forehead. She furiously batted it away.

"OOOOOOOHH," she screamed. Her heart was pumping so hard she thought it would burst out of her chest. "HEEELLLLLP."

She knew that no one could hear her. The wetness from her sweater was dripping down her legs, and her pants felt like clammy bandages around her thighs. She sunk down until she was crouched low and began to rock very slowly. Water lapped against the shore. Reeds swished. An insect buzzed.

She threw her head back and shrieked as loudly as she could. "DARYL!!" she cried, even though she knew it was hopeless. "CAR-RIIEEEE. MARY BETH!" Her voice melted into the water and the endless dark sky.

Zane felt totally and completely alone. As if she were the last girl in California. The last human on earth. She'd grown up in a house teeming with siblings and friends. Maybe her family ignored her half the time, but at least they were there. All through junior high she'd had Carrie and Mary Beth at her side, ready to go along with whatever crazy thing popped into her head. She needed all those other people to bolster her, to prove that Zane Mazerski really did exist. Now she was afraid to merely close her eyes. She was terrified that when she opened them again, there would be nothing there at all.

Zane hugged herself and curled up tight. She'd always wondered what it would feel like if something really happened. And now that she knew, she never wanted to experience anything like it again.

Mary Beth had been searching the entire downtown. The streets, the boat dock, the beach, and the parking lots. She'd even steeled herself to peek into the Watering Hole Tavern and wait outside the row of portable toilets that had been set up for the Fourth of July crowd. She desperately wanted to hook up with Carrie, and, if possible, Zane.

It was almost time to head back, but in spite of her newfound assertiveness, there was only so far that Mary Beth wanted to go. The idea of sneaking back into the bedroom by herself made her never want to go back. What if she got caught? What if Melvin ran out and jumped all over her, instead of just barking his head off? What would she say to Mr. Cates when he asked what had happened to Carrie and Zane? How would she answer when he grilled her about where she had been and if she'd ever snuck out before.

Luckily, Mary Beth spotted Carrie on her fourth search down Main Street . . . just past the Mobil station. Carrie was walking more slowly than Mary Beth had been, but she was also peering into alleyways, staring hard into unlit faces and between parked cars.

"CARRIE!" Mary Beth yelled.

Carrie stopped immediately, then whirled around to find Mary Beth. As soon as she spotted her, she raced across the street. "I've been looking all over for you," Carrie panted.

"Me, too. Did you go to find Phillip?"

Carrie nodded and tears filled her eyes. "He wouldn't talk to me. I know he thinks I'm friends with those jerks who set off the firecracker."

Mary Beth pressed Carrie's shoulder. "You have to explain to him, Carrie."

"I tried. He doesn't want to hear." She stopped to wipe away the tears, then pulled herself together with a deep breath. "Where's Zane?"

"She went on a boat ride with those creepy boys. I wouldn't go."

"Do you think we can find her before we head back? I never should have said for us to meet at the cabin. We should go back in together, like we always have. It could be a disaster if we try to sneak in separately."

"I know."

"I was too upset about Phillip to think." Carrie looked up and down the street. "Do you think we can find Zane?"

Mary Beth checked her watch. "She should be getting back from the boat ride now — at the latest, that is. Let's go down to the dock."

They took off, past the main beach and under the bridge.

"Look," Carrie cried, as soon as they stepped into the boat dock parking lot. "There's a motorboat pulling in." She turned back and grasped Mary Beth's hands. "It's them, I think. We're just in time. Thank God, we're lucky for once tonight."

Mary Beth nodded with relief. "It is them." They tore across the asphalt, around cars with boats on their trailers, past a row of rental slips where boats sat still and unused in the water.

But as soon as they were close to the dock, Carrie and Mary Beth stopped. The most powerful and terrifying sound was coming from the red motorboat boat. It was a moaning, the full-blown retching of a young man who was completely and uncontrollably ill.

"What happened to him?" whispered Carrie.

"He's drunk," Mary Beth said matter-of-factly. "I knew it."

Daryl was being helped out of the boat by the college girl, Matt, and Justin. He was completely limp and moaning as loudly as a sick animal at the zoo. Suddenly, he let out a brutal yell, and the trio backed up, letting Daryl fall onto the asphalt and throw up.

"Ughhh," groaned Carrie.

"Really. Maybe he doesn't look quite so cute to Zane now." Mary Beth led the way past the college kids, onto the wooden dock and over to the boat.

"Hey, keep away from there!" yelled Matt. He had suddenly noticed the girls, while Justin and the college girl were trying to get Daryl back on his feet.

"Where's Zane?" gasped Carrie.

Mary Beth just kept staring into the boat, as if Zane were about to pop out from the ice chest or the inboard motor. "She went out on the boat. I saw her. Maybe she already left." Mary Beth walked across the dock to where Matt was standing. "Where did Zane go? You know, my friend who was with Daryl."

For a moment Matt wouldn't answer, as if Zane were too unimportant to bother with. Finally he started talking. "She's on Cutter's Island."

"Where?"

"That's the island near where we water ski," Carrie said. "What is she doing there?"

"She wanted to get off the boat, so we let her off." Matt shrugged.

"WHAT?"

"Look," Matt threatened. "I happen to have a sick friend here to attend to. I can't even take the time to put the boat in the slip right now, so I certainly can't worry about your friend. Nothing's going to happen to her. If you want, we'll go back later and pick her up."

"When? You left her there all by herself! In the middle of the night! When will you go back and get her?"

Daryl had yelped and collapsed again.

"Whenever I feel like it," Matt yelled back in a furious voice. "Next week if I want to. Look, she didn't have to come with us. I have more important things to think about than your dumb friend right now." Without another look back to Carrie or Mary Beth, he and his friends helped carry Daryl over to their truck.

Chapter 15

Carrie and Mary Beth raced to the first pay phone, which stood just before the entrance under the stone bridge.

"I don't have a quarter," Carrie panicked. Her hands were shaking. She flashed on Stan's lectures about always carrying emergency money. Thank God Stan wasn't the person she had to contact right now.

"Here!" Mary Beth ripped off her tennis shoe and dumped a coin into her palm. She squeezed inside the phone box with Carrie, even though it was littered with empty beer cans, cigarette butts, and burnt-out sparklers. A thick, stale smell lingered and someone had wedged a tiny American flag in the coin return. "Do you remember the Pierces' number?"

Carrie's brain was a furious jumble. None of the important details would come up. Mary Beth recited the number as Carrie shoved the coin in and stabbed at the buttons. "They would have left Zane out there all night," Carrie ranted.

"I know."

"ALL NIGHT! What absolutely disgusting jerks." Carrie pressed the phone to her ear as it began to ring. "Come on," she prayed. "Pick up the phone, Mr. and Mrs. Pierce. Be home." She pounded on the phone. "Please be home. Please!" She waited through five rings. Ten. Twelve. She counted to fourteen before she stamped the ground and slapped the receiver back in its cradle. "There's no answer. What do we do now?"

"We run home and get your dad." Mary Beth looked determined and surprisingly in control. Her eyes were fixed on Carrie and she suddenly looked a lot older than fifteen.

"What am I going to say to him?"

"Just tell him the truth. Carrie, you don't have a choice!"

"Okay." Carrie backed out of the phone booth and banged the door closed. She looked back at the dock. The red motorboat was still tied up at the loading area. There was no one in the parking lot. "What if they come back, M.B.? Daryl and his friends. What if they actually come back to pick Zane up?"

"I'll stay down here at the dock in case the guys come back. You run home by yourself and get your dad. Okay?"

"Okay." Carrie couldn't quite get her legs to move. She pointed down past the dock, at the boat slips. "Why didn't my father show me how to drive my boat?" she cried. "We could have rescued Zane ourselves. Why didn't he do that? He kept saying he would. He kept promising.

But he never showed me. He never even gave me a key."

"It doesn't matter," Mary Beth argued. Even her voice had taken on a firm, grown-up quality. "We have to do what we can. Now go!"

Carrie took off, under and past the bridge, cutting across Main Street and up the dirt road. She was so full of adrenaline that she didn't notice when the hill became steep. Her lungs were on fire. She didn't feel the rocks or ruts, she barely saw the brambles or the trees. She passed the Pierces' cabin, which was completely dark. Not one car had driven by her. She grabbed her father's mailbox and swung herself onto the stairs. Two steps at a time, she climbed up to the cabin.

That was when it hit her — an overwhelming sense of fear and shame. This was nothing like the stifling old feelings she used to have in Stan's house. This was every nerve in her body being twisted and tweaked. Every cell of her skin on edge. Every thought in her brain crisscrossing and making strange connections.

What was her father going to do when he found out how they'd deceived him? He hadn't said absolutely yes to her coming to live with him, but he certainly hadn't said no. More than anything, Carrie had the feeling that he *would* let her move up. It was undefined because everything having to do with divorce was weird and undefined. Her father just wasn't sure how to arrange her move, or definitely put it into words.

But this could change everything, as surely as that firecracker had changed her relationship with Phillip. Thinking about Phillip made her body go frozen again. She still wasn't able to absorb what had happened with Phillip, and yet she was flooded with sadness. It felt like a chunk had been carved out of her. Things with her father really could end this time, as horribly as they'd probably ended with Phillip. This might truly be the moment when everything she'd dreamed of — change, freedom, music, and inspiration — could all explode into a million pieces and never be heard from again.

Carrie took a step onto the porch. Her muscles tensed as she prepared to hear Melvin's watchdog yapping. She stood very still, her heart galloping, her mouth dry. She cringed and waited . . . and waited. For the first time, Melvin didn't bark.

Out of habit, Carrie tiptoed across the porch. The bedroom window was open. The curtain flapped and she suddenly wanted to forget about everything that had happened and climb in. She knew she should hurry, but she also wanted to delay facing her father. She didn't climb in the window. She kept crossing the porch until she realized that a lamp was on in the living room and that her father was in there. Awake.

Carrie froze.

Then it hit her. *He already knows!* He'd gone in to check on them and had finally discovered the empty sleeping bags. He was furious, disappointed . . . sick with worry. He had decided not to let her move up with him and was going over the words he would use to tell her so.

Carrie moved quietly to the door, then stalled again. Trying to crank up her nerve, she peeked in through the living room window. That was when her fear turned to confusion. Disbelief. What she saw was so odd that at first, she wondered if she'd come up to the wrong cabin.

Melvin was passed out on the living room floor, so still that he might have been dead. Finally he shook a little, huffed, and turned over as if he were having a nightmare. He went back to sleep, exhausted, not aware of her at all.

But when she looked past Melvin's worn-out body, she saw the part that really didn't fit together in her brain. Her father and Leslie . . . standing in the middle of the living room. His arms around her waist. Hers around his neck. They kissed, then pulled apart. Leslie giggled and said something that made her father laugh, too. Then they kissed again. And again.

Carrie was absolutely paralyzed now. Light-headed and almost sick. When Mary Beth had mentioned the possibility of her father and Leslie being a couple, Carrie had put the idea on the back shelf of her mind. Part of her said that it didn't matter. Her father was allowed to have his own life. So what if Leslie was young? A classmate at Sherman had a stepmother who wasn't even twenty-one. But most of her said that it simply wasn't true. Her father wouldn't be with some ditsy student. And if he were, he would never be embarrassed by her. He would never hide his real life from Carrie. He would never lie about his girlfriend, pretend that she was some unimportant acquaintance who only needed a place to crash.

Carrie stayed in the shadow by the door and listened. Melvin shuddered again. The radio played very softly. It wasn't until the jazz song ended and the announcer came on that Carrie overheard her father and Leslie.

"Mel. Melvin," Leslie was cooing. She turned back to Carrie's father. "Mel is really out of it. We shouldn't have taken him down to the beach today. I'm telling you, fireworks are total dog trauma. Mel won't be himself for days."

"Melvin," her dad called. "Wake up and keep watch, old guy. Don't fail me now."

Leslie snuggled and sighed. "Maybe I should just go back out on the porch now. What if Mel doesn't warn us. The girls usually come back by one-thirty."

"Maybe you should, Les. I don't want to have to start explaining now. It's hard enough for me to talk to Carrie as it is. I'm not prepared for this full-time father stuff. Thanks for putting up with this."

Leslie punched him. "You'll pay. Don't worry. I'll find a way to get my revenge." She giggled again.

"I bet you will."

Carrie leaned her head back against the cabin wall, unable to listen to any more. She was dizzy, breathless. The crisscrossing in her brain was gone, replaced by dead air. She felt as if all the blood had been sucked out of her. They had never fooled her father, not for a single sneak attack. He was just as happy to let them sneak out and run downtown, so that he could spend time alone with Leslie. He didn't care what they did, or what kind of trouble they got into. He didn't want to help her find a new road now that she was sixteen. He just hoped she'd disappear down some blind alley.

Leslie was padding across the living room now on her way to the kitchen. When she passed by the front door, Carrie flattened against the wall. More than anything she didn't want to face Leslie. Not now. She didn't want to face her father, either. She didn't know how she could accuse her father of being dishonest, when she'd been deceiving him just as thoroughly. At least she didn't have to think about how she had disappointed him, because she couldn't deal with the way he had disappointed her.

The kitchen light went on and the refrigerator door opened. Melvin lifted his weary head. Carrie took a slow step away from the corner and the dog looked right at her. She took another step. Melvin finally started barking when Carrie bolted across the porch and started running full speed down the steps and into the street.

Mary Beth couldn't stand waiting. Time seemed to be moving in reverse as she looked up and down the dock, from Carrie's striped boat to the sparkly red motorboat. Water slapped wood. Planks creaked under her feet. She felt as if she'd been waiting all her life. Waiting to speak up, waiting to turn sixteen. Well, the waiting was finally over.

Something had happened to Mary Beth over the last two weeks. Maybe it was being away from her mother. Maybe it was the sun and the river and the wide-open sky. Maybe it was the realization that Zane and Carrie might be bolder and flashier than she was, but they certainly weren't any smarter.

"Zane," Mary Beth swore as she stomped down the ramp that led along the boat slips. Because Zane was so forceful and wild, Mary Beth had always assumed that she was the one to follow. Mary Beth never considered that she might have as much going for her as Zane. Maybe more. If only she could trust her perception and her brain, her sense of when to say yes and when to say no.

She stood in front of Carrie's boat and stared at the single plastic dinosaur still taped to the steering wheel. The slips smelled of rotting wood and fuel. Holding tight to the side of Carrie's boat, Mary Beth stepped in. When the boat rocked beneath her, she lurched forward, tumbling onto the bench that had been covered with music paper. She crawled to the front and found the glove compartment.

"Darn!" It was locked. Mary Beth slammed it with her fist. She peeled off the plastic dinosaur and tried to pick the lock with the point of its tail. Finally she hauled off and kicked the compartment with the bottom of her shoe.

The compartment door flopped open. Inside were candy bars, lubricating oil, a can opener, and gas receipts. She dug around, flinging the paper and Mars Bars onto the boat floor. Then she found what she was looking for. A flashlight. A boat manual. An extra ignition key.

She read the manual more carefully than she'd ever read any spy novel or book of fairy tales. Illuminating diagram after diagram, she stared back and forth between the pages and the boat. First, she identified the parts, as if this were an experiment with her chemistry set. She pushed in the key. Pulled out the choke. The boat rumbled to life, then shut down just as quickly. Finally she slammed the engine with her fist and it began to purr. Softly. Evenly. She put the boat in neutral, remembered the simulator in Driver's Ed., and held tightly to the wheel.

She forced the shift lever down. The boat lurched forward with such force that she almost ran into the dock. So she let up and it put-putted away from the slip, away from the red boat, and out into the dark, shiny water. Mary Beth looked up at the stars. She got her bearings from the skyline and the outline of the shore. She wasn't exactly sure how to get to Cutter's Island, but she figured that if she trusted her instincts for once, she just might make it.

"MARY BETH!!!"
Carrie arrived at the dock only to hear her own voice come back to her. Her legs were screaming and there was a painful ache from her

stomach to her neck. She wept. She sat on the dock and cried, the tears running down her face like rapids. She wailed with full voice, since she knew no one was around to hear. This night was turning out to be such a mass of twists and turns that she half expected the mountains to tumble down on top of her or the river to flow upstream.

"EMMMMM BEEEEEEEE!!!!!!" Carrie threw back her head. "WHERE ARE YOU???"

Carrie knew that the college boys hadn't come back, since their boat was still tied to the dock. Mary Beth had probably gotten frightened waiting alone and decided to follow her. Now they had lost one another, and who knew when they would meet up again?

And this whole time, while Mr. Cates kissed Leslie and Mary Beth roamed around Watson River looking for her, Zane sat on the horrible island, deserted and dumped. Carrie told herself that she was sixteen now. She should know what to do. But she could only think that if this was what it meant to turn sixteen, she would rather go back to knee socks and training bras.

"WHAT AM I SUPPOSED TO DO?" she screamed to the starry sky. She was answered by the slap of water and more tears dripping down her cheeks.

She wanted someone to come and fix this whole night, she realized. Her father . . . no, not her father. God, she would have settled for her mother or Stan. But as she looked up and down the dock, across the parking lot and past the bridge, she saw no one. Not even a shadow.

"Okay," she said, standing up and stalking away from the dock. She ran again. Her legs were numb by this time, her muscles like scalding water. She raced down Main Street, which was almost deserted. She turned onto a dirt lane, past patchy lawns and cats out on midnight cruises, and finally stopped in front of the only other place she could think of to go. Phillip's house.

The house was dark, except for the room over the garage. Carrie had no idea if that room was Phillip's, or if he would even talk to her if she did find him. The only thing she knew was that Zane was still on Cutter's Island. Her father wasn't going to change things. She had to handle this on her own.

She scavenged for small stones and started pitching them up at the window.

I'll break a window and get arrested, she told herself. That would be the perfect ending to this night. Zane would be alone in the middle of the river. Mary Beth would be wandering around town somewhere. Her father would be with Leslie. And she would be in jail.

Carrie took a shaky breath and pitched again. She tossed and tossed. Her arm was getting tired and she could barely see. Half her stones hit the garage door or fell into the neighbor's rosebushes. Carrie was beginning to think that no one lived in that lit room at all when the curtains finally parted and a dark, curly headed boy appeared behind the window frame.

"Phillip," Carrie breathed. The sadness came rushing back to her.

Phillip stared down suspiciously. He shoved the window open and called in a muted but threatening voice, "Who's out there?"

The anger in his voice cut like glass. "Phillip, it's me. Carrie."

He moved closer to the window. "What are you doing here?" He leaned out. "Is anyone with you?"

"It's just me." Carrie was calling as quietly as she could, but she was still afraid of waking Phillip's parents, or half the neighborhood. "Please come down. I'm in trouble. Zane's in trouble. Please. I need help."

Phillip remained in the window just long enough for Carrie to wonder if he would ever budge from there. Then the curtains clapped shut. A moment later he was trotting down a set of outdoor stairs that ran along the side of the garage. He wore a Watson High baseball shirt and hiking shorts. His feet were bare and his hair fell over his forehead. When he came to meet her he looked up and down the dark street, as if he thought there might be people hiding and waiting to jump out.

"What's wrong?" he asked flatly. "It's pretty late."

"I know. I wouldn't be here if it wasn't an emergency. It's Zane. She went with those jerks that threw the firecracker. They ditched her on Cutter's Island. She's there all by herself."

"They left her there? In the middle of the night?" Phillip's mouth fell open with astonishment.

"Yes. Can I use your rowboat to go get her? I'll row it myself. I'll bring it right back. I promise."

Phillip stared and took a step closer to her. Then he pointed down to the boat. "Yes. Of course," he rambled, still amazed. "If your friend really is in trouble."

Not looking at him, Carrie ran past the garage and toward the water. She picked up one of the oars that sat on the dock and looked at the boat. She'd never rowed before, and she had no idea how to get to the island. But she would do it, she told herself. She had to do it. She started to get into the boat.

"What are you doing?" Phillip called as he jogged down to join her. "You can't do this yourself."

"Yes I can. I have to." Carrie grabbed the other oar and reached for the rope.

Phillip grabbed it away from her. "Let me help you."

"No," Carrie insisted, starting to cry again. "I'll find her myself."

Phillip climbed in the boat and sat down next to her. Carrie was almost afraid to look into his eyes, but she felt his hand on hers as she grasped the oar.

"We'll find her together," he said.

Then silently they pushed away from the dock and began to row.

Chapter 16

Zane was crouched on the shore of Cutter's Island. At first she was indistinguishable from the clumps of reeds and scrubby mounds of oak. The pink streak in her hair didn't illuminate her, nor did her long earring, her red Reeboks, or her spandex pants. It was too dark to see any of the flags Zane usually sent up to get herself noticed. Too dark. Too wet. Too lonely. And too late.

As soon as Carrie's motorboat scratched bottom, Mary Beth jumped out. Up to her thighs in water and reeds, she wrapped the tow rope around a bush, then waded furiously up to shore to find Zane.

"ZANE!" Mary Beth screamed.

At first she only heard the wind ripping through the grass and the water lapping against the side of the boat, but finally Mary Beth saw her. It was the quietest entrance Zane had ever made. She simply stood up from the hollow she had found between a bramble and two short trees.

"Is someone there? Mary Beth? You found me. You came. Oh. Thank you. Oh." Zane shivered.

Mary Beth rushed over to Zane. "Here, put this on," she said, flinging off her sweater. "Your sweater is all wet."

Zane just stared at Mary Beth, her eyes full of gratitude and affection. "M.B., I'm sorry. I'm so sorry about what I said about not being friends anymore. I didn't mean it. I could never mean it. I get so boy crazy. I'm such a jerk. Will you ever forgive me?"

"Of course I forgive you. You have to forgive crazy people. Now put this on."

"I'm okay."

"Zane, put it on. It's your sweater."

Zane took the sweater, but before putting it on she threw herself at Mary Beth, hugging her fiercely. "Why do I get so carried away with dumb things? Why didn't I see that those guys were awful? Why didn't I listen to you, M.B.?"

"I don't know, Zaney," Mary Beth soothed. "Maybe I never said very much worth listening to before."

Zane hugged her again. "Oh, Mary Beth, thanks. I never thought anything would happen. I never thought anything really could happen. I never thought . . ." She finally separated herself and both girls sat down on the shore. They listened to the water, Zane's head resting on Mary Beth's shoulder. It was almost as if they were too tired to get in the boat and drive back.

"Where's Carrie?" Zane finally asked.

That was when they saw the rowboat cutting

across the river, slicing toward the island. At the same time, Zane and Mary Beth stood up. The boat swayed through patches of light, quiet except for the swishing of the strokes. The rhythm of the rowing was musical and even. As the boat floated up to the island, Zane and Mary Beth saw that Carrie pulled one oar while Phillip Davison pulled the other.

The four of them looked at one another. So much had happened that there seemed very little to say. Carrie and Phillip stayed in the rowboat, while Mary Beth and Zane stumbled through shallow water to join them.

"I found her," Mary Beth said proudly.

"So this is where you went." Carrie rubbed her eyes. "How did you get my boat going?"

Mary Beth shrugged. "I figured it out."

"Zane, are you okay?"

"I'm okay," Zane whispered. "Now."

Carrie let her face drop into her hand, then looked up at Phillip. He was glancing back and forth between her and Zane. She wasn't sure what he was thinking, or if she could make sense of much of anything on this insane night. She felt as if she'd been battered and bruised, run fifty miles, and lost her best friend. But at least his eyes were letting her in.

Zane took hold of the side of Phillip's boat. "Your dad must know now," Zane said to Carrie. "I ruined everything. It's all my fault."

Carrie bit back a surprising flash of tears. "There's more to it than my dad finding out. I'll tell you everything later."

Zane wrinkled up her face, then shivered. At last, she looked right at Phillip. "I'm sorry. I can be kind of a jerk sometimes."

Phillip stared back at her. There was no hardness in his face now, only curiosity and concern.

Moonlight made Zane's face look almost innocent. It was one of those rare times when she looked like she really would be the last of the girls to turn sixteen. "You guys came to find me, too. Thank you, Phillip. After the way I acted toward you, you probably wanted to leave me here for the rest of my life."

Phillip cracked a smile and a dimple dug into his cheek. "I'd better not answer that."

"Maybe we can start over," Zane said. "I feel like I should start this whole summer over." She stuck out her hand for Phillip to shake. "I'm Zane. I'd like to meet you. I really am a friend of Carrie's." She glanced at Carrie. "At least I hope I still am. I'm her crazy friend. Everybody has to have a crazy friend, right? And I'm not a friend of those guys who threw that firecraker in your father's store. I'm sorry. I'm really sorry."

Phillip shook Zane's hand, then took up his oar again. "We'd better get back. We're all going to be in enough trouble already. Can you make it?"

Mary Beth nodded. She and Zane climbed in the motorboat. "Follow me," Phillip said. "You can dock your boat behind my house and then take it to the slip tomorrow."

Like two mismatched couples in a crew race, both boats slid into the water and took off.

* * *

Carrie and Phillip sat in the rowboat about two hundred feet off shore. The sky was velvet blue. The water rolled softly and the unused oars clacked against the side of the boat. They could see Zane and Mary Beth on Phillip's dock. The girls were huddled together, waiting for Carrie, but in no obvious hurry.

For the first time since Carrie'd walked Phillip home, she felt that they were alone. Really alone. No friends lurking in the distance to spoil things. No ice cream store. No guitar. Nothing but the two of them, the boat, the water, and the sky. She was exhausted, and yet his company gave her a second wind. She felt as if she'd stayed up through a sixteen-day blackout and was finally getting a glimpse of the sun.

"Hi," she said.

"Hi."

"I feel like Zane, like I should start over and get to know you again."

"Are you like Zane?"

"No, I don't think so. But she is one of my best friends."

"And those guys who threw the fire-cracker — "

"Are not, never have been, never will be friends of mine! Or of Zane's again. I hope."

"Good." He kicked at the oar. "Zane's not the only one who can act like a jerk. And I don't just mean those college guys, either." When she laughed he stretched his arms up to the sky. Then he turned to face her. His eyes took in every inch of her face again, as if he could find everything he'd ever needed to know there. "I don't know why I was so quick to think you were one of them."

That current was flowing back and forth. Carrie was hooked and unable to move. "I'm not."

"I know." He smoothed her hair away from her eyes. Then he slid even closer. Neither of them looked away. They weren't self-conscious or embarrassed. Maybe it was too late, and they'd been through too much to be anything but straightforward.

"You know I'm leaving in a few days," Carrie said.

Alarm covered his handsome face. "But you're coming back. I thought you were moving up north with your dad."

"I guess I've changed my mind."

"But you said he was going to fix everything for you."

Carrie dropped her head on his shoulder, which was hard and warm under the soft layer of cotton. "I guess he isn't. Maybe it was dumb to ever think that one person could fix everything for you."

"One person can change a whole summer, though."

"Who do you mean?"

Phillip touched her chin, causing her to lift her face and look at him again. His eyes had turned as soft as felt. "Who do you think I mean?"

"I thought you didn't want to talk to me anymore."

"That was just because . . . Oh, never mind."

"What?"

He cleared his throat, as if this was difficult for him to say. "Meeting you was important to me. Scary. You're different from me. You come from a different place. You don't assume that things have to stay the way they are."

"No, I just wait for other people to make them better — "

Phillip interrupted her. "That's why I got so mad when I thought you were friends with those jerks in the store. I couldn't stand having something so important fall through for me. I couldn't stand it if you turned out to be just another summer person."

"Why should I turn out to be like that?"

Phillip didn't answer for a moment. It was as if he'd never considered that things could be any different. "I don't know. Maybe I'm like my dad. I think that things have always been one way, so that's the way they have to stay."

"They don't."

"Maybe they don't." Phillip glanced at the dock, then back to Carrie. He wound his hands around hers. "Maybe I could visit you in L.A., go look at colleges there. Maybe I could still go to that workshop in San Jose, and visit you afterward. My dad might have a fit . . ."

"So?"

"So, maybe I could do it anyway."

"Maybe you could."

"My counselor told me that they have a great

ecology department at a school in Long Beach. Is that near where you live?"

"It's not far."

"I could use the money I saved from last summer."

"I could even come back and visit you here."

Carrie noticed suddenly that Zane and Mary Beth had stood up. They were standing on the dock, waving to tell her that it was definitely time to go.

"It's late. I know," Phillip said.

"I'd better go."

"I know."

"But we'll see each other again."

"There's lots of things that could change."

Neither moved to pick up an oar. Finally Phillip put both hands on Carrie's shoulders. She touched his face and then she wasn't sure if she kissed him, or he kissed her. At the same time they both closed their eyes and came together. Everything else disappeared. No more fathers. No more cabins or boats. No rivers or electric-blue swimming pools. Just her and Phillip, as fluid and natural together as the water and the sky.

They rowed back to the dock in silence. When they parted there was nothing else to say. It had all been said and they both understood perfectly. Carrie slowly climbed onto the dock. She joined Zane and Mary Beth and only turned back once to look at him. Phillip was still standing there, watching her and smiling.

* * *

When she was finally back at the cabin, Carrie was glad she'd decided to walk home. She was glad that for once she'd taken some time to think and consider, rather than letting her feelings explode all over the place. She sat in the living room with her father. Zane and Mary Beth had gone to sleep. So had Leslie. Even poor old Melvin was sacked out.

"I kept thinking about what your mother would say," her father was explaining. He looked exhausted. When the girls hadn't come home by two, he'd finally gone out to look for them. They'd all met up on the road leading to the cabin. "I didn't know what you would think of me. My life is not exactly like Stan's. I haven't spent that much time with you, Carrie. I guess I'm not sure what to expect of you, and what you expect of me."

Carrie sat very still. Her brain wasn't crisscrossing, she wasn't crying or feeling like she had to break away. She was simply going over what had happened and trying to sort it out. "I would have understood about Leslie."

"Would you?" He looked skeptical.

"Maybe I wouldn't."

"Carrie, I think you might have had a lot of unrealistic ideas about me. I didn't want to disappoint you. And that's just what I did."

"Didn't you worry about us when you knew we were sneaking out? Didn't you want to bother stopping us?"

He rubbed his face with his hands. His eyes

were puffy and even his mustache had drooped. "I guess in some ways I didn't want to bother. It was easier to go on with my life, the part I didn't think you'd approve of." He held Carrie's hand, squeezing it hard. "But I also wanted you to have freedom. I wanted to treat you like an adult."

"But I'm not an adult. I'm sixteen. *You're* supposed to be the adult."

He shook his head. "Carrie, I don't feel like an adult half the time, either."

"But didn't you worry? Didn't you worry that something would happen?"

"I thought you hated the way Stan always worried."

Carrie was suddenly so confused that she began to laugh. "I'm sorry," she explained. "I know this isn't funny. None of it's funny. But I'm so tired and it's been a pretty crazy day."

"For me, too. Actually, I think I understand. If I wasn't so tired, maybe I could laugh, too. Maybe someday we'll both be able to laugh about this." He hugged her and sighed. "Why don't we go to sleep? We can talk more tomorrow."

"Promise?" Carrie asked, pulling back and looking right at him. "You won't have all your other friends to talk to instead?"

He closed his eyes, his tired face showing hurt and regret. "I promise."

"Okay." She got up and slowly walked across the living room. Her limbs and her head were heavy. It was still dark outside. It had cooled down and there was a calm stillness in the air.

"Carrie," he called. She had stopped in the hallway and was bending down to pat Melvin. "Will you come stay with me again next summer? Maybe we can do a better job next time. I love you, kid."

"I'm not a kid, Dad. I may not be an adult, but I'm not a kid."

He smiled sadly. "I know. But you're *my* kid. I hope this summer hasn't been a waste. I do love you."

For the first time since they'd returned to the cabin, tears pulled at Carrie's throat. "I love you, Dad," she whispered. She petted Melvin one more time and went around the hall.

She closed the bedroom door behind her. For a moment she listened to Mary Beth's tired breathing. Zane was tossing on her mattress on the floor, making tiny sounds like a little kid. The room was warm, even though a breeze ruffled the curtains and the window was still wide open.

Carrie sat on the edge of the bed and looked at Mary Beth wrapped up in her sleeping bag. Mary Beth looked different. Maybe it was because she no longer hugged her pillow or the stillness with which she slept now. Something had changed. For all of them. It seemed as if the three of them had been living in that room for ages. A lifetime. This summer had been a lot of things, but certainly not a waste.

Carrie quietly unzipped her sleeping bag and crawled in. Even though every muscle in her body was worn out, her mind was still going. Not crisscrossing. Leapfrogging. From one clear thought to another. Her father. Leslie. Stan. Her mom. Going home and starting school again. Zane and Mary Beth. This town and this cabin and this room.

. . . and Phillip. It was when she started thinking about Phillip that everything went soft and relaxed. Phillip was everything she'd hoped would happen when she turned sixteen. Carrie felt herself smile as she finally closed her eyes and drifted off to sleep.

Chapter 17

"Can you believe that?"

"Some people shouldn't even be allowed to go out in public."

"You're telling me."

"We would never do anything like that."

"Not me, anyway. Maybe you two. But not me."

"You'd never do anything crazy, Zane."

"Impossible."

"None of us would."

"Never."

"Never again. Well, maybe never again."

Carrie leaned over the Taco Bell bench and strained to get a better look. They were discussing a table full of seniors, some wearing Sherman High T-shirts, all engaged in a no-holds-barred "full meal deal" food fight. Fajitas were flying. Salsa spattered. Soft tacos and nachos were being dropped down the backs of shirts and on the tops of heads. The concrete under their table looked like feeding time at The San Diego Zoo.

"Well," Carrie sighed, "welcome back to L.A."

Zane made her Godzilla face, and they all started laughing. Carrie wasn't sure why it was so funny, but it was. It felt good to laugh at things. Carrie'd realized when she first got home that she could either laugh or be in a constant state of anxiety and tears. Somehow she had a different perspective now on the cars roaring by, the smog building up, the people crowding around, and the buildings stretching everywhere. At sixteen Carrie knew that however rough things got in the valley, they weren't any rougher than anywhere else in the world.

"So, M.B., your mother is really going to let us go?" Zane wondered, as she stretched her arm across the table to steal some of Carrie's chips. Bracelets jangled. Zane's new nail design, pink and yellow polka dots, glistened under the bright sun. "Just the three of us?"

"Sure," Mary Beth said. "A whole day at Disneyland. I think she wanted me to say I'd start my own business or go on a safari. But I told her Disneyland was where I wanted to go when my birthday finally arrived. And she said okay."

"What about getting your license?"

Mary Beth stretched her arms over her head. They'd been back for four days, but her tan was still nut-brown and she was covered with freckles. "She wants me to go the morning of my birthday. As soon as the D.M.V. opens."

"And are you going to?"

"Actually, I think I will."

"Amazing," Zane sighed. She bobbed up and did a little mock imitation of a cheerleader doing a yell. "I thought you weren't in any hurry to start driving."

"I'm not. It's just that you guys are coming with me and I want to make you get up really early."

"No!"

"Do we have to?" Zane complained.

"Yes," Mary Beth answered fiercely. "You owe me one."

Zane shrugged. "Oh well. I guess Disneyland will be worth it. We can sneak all over Tom Sawyer's Island, shake up that rope bridge, hide in Davey Crockett's fort, and see what boys come by."

"Zane," Mary Beth warned, pointing her finger. "If you go with me, the craziest thing you're going to do is go on Mr. Toad's Wild Ride."

Zane started to argue, then smiled and shrugged. "Okay. So maybe I get carried away. But we're going on Space Mountain even if it makes you puke."

"Okay." Mary Beth laughed.

Carrie nudged Zane. "Are you sure you want a whole day of cartoon characters? Think about it, Zane."

Zane buried her face in her hands. "Noooo! What if I run into Popeye?"

"Don't worry," Mary Beth told her. "I don't think Popeye is a Disney character. But I still think you should stick with me and Carrie."

"Maybe I should." Zane raised her head again, flung back her earring, and threatened. "Remember, you can't tell anyone. No one at Sherman can know what happened this summer. We can only talk about it among the three of us. Promise?"

The three pairs of eyes made contact.

"Promise."

"Promise."

They all sat back for a moment, feeling as connected as a tightly knit family or a secret clan. Carrie hummed softly. Mary Beth picked at the nachos. Zane watched the cars. The food fight next door had ended and the seniors were cleaning up their mess.

"So, did anybody tell their parents?" Zane finally asked in a lower voice. Their silly mood had dissolved. Now they leaned in and gazed at one another with serious eyes. "Nothing but the truth here."

Mary Beth shook her head. "My mother would have been ecstatic that something exciting had finally happened to me. But I wanted to keep it to myself. I told her some of the stuff we did — I just left a few major things out."

"Carrie?"

Carrie twisted her napkin and sighed. "My mom and Stan kept grilling me about my father. I didn't tell them much, except that I'd decided not to move up there. When they heard that, the pressure really lightened up. Stan and I actually had one of our first non-yelling conversations."

"About what?"

"About what kind of chlorine is best for the swimming pool."

"Really?"

Carrie laughed. "No. Not really, M.B. He came to tell me that he was glad I'd decided not to move. Maybe we could be friends. It was totally embarrassing. But he gave me a birthday present. Guitar lessons. Of course, they're *classical* guitar lessons, but he was trying." Carrie nudged Zane. "What about you?"

"Well . . . " Zane hesitated, made a funny face, and then finally admitted. "I actually did tell my parents."

"You did!"

"Zane!"

"I glossed over some parts, like what a total bozo I was. But I wanted to see how they'd react."

"And?"

"They actually got mad. In the middle of it one of my brothers broke the blender and my sister spilled paint all over the kitchen floor. My mom didn't even notice them. She was too busy yelling at me."

Mary Beth lurched forward and knocked over the salsa. "So what happened? How come you're not grounded?"

Zane shrugged. "They said I had to use my own judgment and that they know I would make mistakes. They just hoped I'd learned something."

"That's all they said?"

"And if I ever did anything like that again, they'd kill me."

They all nodded.

"It seems like it happened a million years ago," Carrie said wistfully. She pulled up her knees and hugged them, gazing out at the traffic, into the black glass of the bank building right across the street. In some ways she could hardly believe there had ever been a Watson River. Her perceptions of the place had changed so dramatically from what she'd expected, to what she understood now. It was the same with her father. Letting go of her perfect idea of him almost made it seem as if he no longer existed. And yet, it allowed the rest of her life to come into clearer focus.

"A million years," Zane scoffed. She grinned at Mary Beth. "She already has a letter and she acts like it's a million years. Give me a break. I guess that's what happens when you turn sixteen."

Carrie blushed. She'd read them every word of Phillip's first letter. Well, almost every word. Carrie had done some strategic editing, but not much. There wasn't really anything now about her relationship with Phillip that she didn't want to share with the whole world. Besides, when Carrie read about what he wrote about the river and the town and what had happened since they'd left, she could almost smell the trees and hear the water tumbling down the rocks. The good part of their summer seemed to be right there, in those pages.

"He might come and visit at the end of the summer," Carrie told Zane and Mary Beth.

"Really?"

"After he goes to this workshop in San Jose. He finally talked to his father and they're finding somebody else to work in August. So Phillip's going to try and come visit me after he's done."

"Did you send him the tape of your new song?" Zane asked.

Carrie nodded.

"Well?" Zane banged the tabletop. "Did he like it?"

"I liked it," Mary Beth offered. "I thought it was the best one you've ever written."

"I don't know yet if he liked it." Carrie said, laughing again and flicking some lettuce at Zane. "But when I find out, you two will be the first to know."

"We'd better be." Zane grabbed the half-eaten nachos that sat in front of Mary Beth. "So what are we going to do today? After telling my folks what happened, I'm forbidden from going to the beach with my brothers."

They all groaned.

"We could go to the mall."

"Hang out at the tennis courts."

"Climb the fences around Balboa park."

"Listen to music and make Mexican food."

"Can't we think of anything else?" Carrie asked, and she knew from the looks on her friends' faces that they understood her objection. Those were all pre-sixteen activities. The second part of this summer had to be as different as she was now.

"We could study the driver's manual."

"Go over to Sherman High and check things out."

"See if anything new is going into the music room," said Carrie.

"The library," chimed in Mary Beth.

Zane got one of her wild looks and added, "The cafeteria!"

That was all it took. Nachos took to the air. Bits of lettuce and tortilla and cheese whizzed across the table. Chips soared like little flying saucers. Tomatoes splatted and ice was flung with perfect aim. Mary Beth went on the attack, while Zane protected herself, and Carrie just sat back and laughed and laughed.

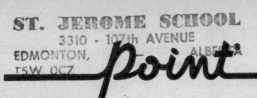

Other books you will enjoy, about real kids like you!

☐ 42365-7 **Blind Date** R.L. Stine $2.50

☐ 41248-5 **Double Trouble**
Barthe DeClements and
Christopher Greimes $2.75

☐ 41432-1 **Just a Summer Romance**
Ann M. Martin $2.50

☐ 40935-2 **Last Dance** Caroline B. Cooney $2.50

☐ 41549-2 **The Lifeguard** Richie Tankersley Cusick $2.50

☐ 33829-3 **Life Without Friends**
Ellen Emerson White $2.75

☐ 40548-9 **A Royal Pain** Ellen Conford $2.50

☐ 41823-8 **Simon Pure** Julian F. Thompson $2.75

☐ 40927-1 **Slumber Party** Christopher Pike $2.50

☐ 41186-1 **Son of Interflux** Gordon Korman $2.50

☐ 41513-7 **The Tricksters** Margaret Mahy $2.95

☐ 41546-8 **Yearbook II: Best All-Around Couple**
Melissa Davis $2.50

PREFIX CODE
0-590-

**Available wherever you buy books...
or use the coupon below.**